Friends, enemies

Friends, enemies

ROSIE RUSHTON

HYPERION Paperbacks

New York

Copyright © 2003 by Rosie Rushton

First published in the U.K. 2003 as *Friends, Enemies, and Other Tiny Problems.* Reprinted by permission of Piccadilly Press. All rights reserved. No part of this book may be reproduced or transmitted in any form or by any means, electronic or mechanical, including photocopying, recording, or by any information storage and retrieval system, without written permission from the publisher. For information address Hyperion Books for Children, 114 Fifth Avenue, New York, New York 10011-5690.

Printed in the United States of America

First U. S. Paperback edition, 2006

3 5 7 9 10 8 6 4 2

Library of Congress Cataloging-in-Publication Data on file.

ISBN 0-7868-5178-3 (pbk.)

Visit www.hyperionteens.com

With grateful thanks to the following pupils of Weatherhead High School, Wallasey, for their advice on what it's like to make friends and break friends: Sarah Norris, Helen Minting, Kerryanne Price, Dizzy Hobson, Hannah Eisenberg, Mary Eisenberg, Rebecca Cutts, Laura Jamieson, Suzanne Salisbury, Jennifer Pierce, Siân Evans, Lindsey Evans, Sophie McKibben, Fiona Worral, Laura Kelly, Rebecca Webster, Hannah Woo, Steph Fletcher, Michelle Akehurst, and Natalie McNamee.

I am also indebted to the pupils of Campion School, Bugbroke, Northampton, and to my long-suffering agent, Jane Judd, for her flashes of insight and sense of humor; and to Brenda Gardner and Yasemin Uçar for putting up with my moans on the days I decided I would never write again!

Prologue

I can't believe it's a year ago today that everything began to go horribly wrong. Of course, Ella, who reads the horoscope every day and who believes in ghosts and gremlins and practically every other airy-fairy thing you can think of, said it was because Venus and Mars were opposing each other in Saturn—or something like that, anyway.

Pippa, whose whole life is organized down to the tiniest detail, and who has already planned the date of her wedding (July 4, 2013, if you're interested) said it was because the rest of us were far too soft and couldn't see what was happening right under our noses.

Christy didn't say much at all, but then Christy lives in a dreamworld, composing music and choreographing imaginary people in imaginary ballets.

And Hannah? Well, I guess Hannah made us all feel guilty. That goes without saying. Hannah was good at doing that. Almost as good as she was at whining. Writing it down in black and white makes me feel really mean—after all, it was me who got her into our crowd in the first place.

As the others kept reminding me.

If we hadn't tried to be kind and forgiving, it would never have happened. I guess we were stupid to miss the warning signs. The signs that started the night of the party. . . .

Friends, enemies

* 1 *
Party Politics

"**You've done what?**"

Ella slammed her can of lemonade down on the table and stared at me openmouthed.

"I've invited Hannah to the party tomorrow," I gabbled, taking a deep breath and trying to make it sound as if I'd pulled off the social coup of the year.

"Tory! You idiot! How could you be so stupid?" Ella pulled at the elastic bands holding her pigtails in place and shook her long, blond hair free. It was something she always did when brewing for an argument.

Pippa raised her eyes for a brief second from her plate of chips and mouthed, "I told you so!" behind Ella's back. The way Pippa is always right can be hugely sickening at times.

"You weren't even meant to tell her about the party!" Ella went on, ripping the peel off her orange. "We made a pact, remember?"

"I know, but my . . ." I began, and then thought

better of it. I knew exactly what Ella would say if I admitted I was simply doing what my mother told me to do.

"Well, you'll just have to un-invite her!" Ella declared, blowing a strand of blond hair out of her eye. "She is not coming and that's final!"

"Who's not coming where?" Christy, who always takes twice as long as the rest of us to choose her lunch, sauntered up to the table with a baked potato and a plate of wilting salad.

Ella sighed impatiently. "Tory's only gone and invited Hannah to the party," she said.

"Hannah? Which Hannah?"

Christy is a lovely person but she lives on a totally different planet from the rest of us.

"*Which Hannah?*" Ella mimicked Christy's bewildered tones. "Who has been trailing around behind us for the past heaven-knows-how-long?"

A look of recognition flashed across Christy's freckled face.

"Oh—you mean Hannah Soper," she said, nodding calmly.

"Hannah So-Pathetic, more like!" Ella retorted and looked expectantly at Pippa and Christy. Christy burst out laughing, and even Pippa giggled behind her hand until I kicked her under the table.

"That girl is *so* not us!" Ella ranted on.

"Of course she's not us, she's her!" Pippa argued. Pippa's like that—particular about the tiniest detail. "Anyway, she's not that bad," she went on, flicking her braid over her shoulder and making a belated attempt at sticking up for me. "Okay, so she's a bit wet but . . ."

"Wet? She's positively sodden!" Ella spluttered. "She's always moaning about something, and when she's not whining, she's following us 'round like some lost puppy. Typical Capricorn, of course—no guts!"

Ella was even more keen on guts than she was on astrology. She would tolerate you liking hip-hop instead of R & B, she'd even put up with people who weren't high-flying, straight-A types like her; but show the slightest tendency toward wimpishness, and you were out. Which was why, the year before, when I first got into her set, I'd had to remove a giant spider from her schoolbag without flinching; present a petition to our Head of Year saying that we thought the "no earrings, only studs" rule was outmoded and showed gross discrimination against the fashion-conscious; and skive off Biology to go and buy chocolate—all to prove that I was gutsy. Even now, two years later, there were times when I got the distinct impression that Ella was still testing me.

"You should have just told her straight," she stressed to me. "This is our birthday treat and it's just for our gang."

"Oh, come on!" Christy protested, so strongly that we all turned in amazement. Christy's usually too immersed in her own dreamworld to engage with anything anyone else is talking about. "We couldn't do that—it would be so mean!"

"And," added Pippa, "she *is* part of our gang. Sort of."

"I suppose," said Ella somewhat sullenly. "But she won't be for much longer if she doesn't get her act together!"

She glanced around the crowded cafeteria.

"Where is she, anyway? She's usually stuck to our sides like glue."

"First aid room," I said without thinking. "She had a splinter."

"I rest my case!" cried Ella triumphantly. "You really want someone as feeble as that hanging around tomorrow night? I don't think so."

I said nothing. I know Ella—she can breathe fire and brimstone one day and be all sweetness and light the next.

"It's not Tory's fault," Pippa butted in. "Her mum made her invite Hannah."

This was true, but not exactly something I wanted the whole world to know. The thing about Pippa is that she always says it like it is. No messing.

"Your mother can't tell you what to do—you're going to be fourteen!" protested Ella, looking aghast. "That is so not on!"

Just because she has normal parents, she forgets that some of us are not quite so fortunate. Mind you, I only had myself to blame; if I hadn't agreed to teach my mum how to surf the Internet, she would never have found the Friends Reunited site, and would never have caught up with Hannah's mum, who was at school with her back in the Dark Ages and who had just moved to Westbeach.

"What a coincidence!" Mum had cried, after telling me of her amazing discovery. "Angela was in my class at school and—would you believe it—she has a daughter your age! And guess what?"

I hadn't bothered to respond. With my mother,

there is no need, because she never pauses for long enough to hear your reply.

"She's going to be starting at Elmdean Upper next week—in your class!"

She had gazed at me as if expecting me to jump up and down in excitement.

"Won't that be lovely?" she had enthused. "Angela was quite a character at school as I recall, and I just know you and Hannah will be best buddies in no time!"

My mother is a stranger to logical thought processes.

Most parents would have left it at that. Not my mother. When Mrs. Soper told her that Hannah was really nervous about starting a new school, my mother had the audacity to phone my school and say that Hannah was a friend of the family, and that I'd be thrilled to look after her until she found her feet.

Which was why for the whole of the summer term, Mrs. Temple, our Head of Year, gave me the role of Hannah's minder. Which meant that either she had to hang out with us lot or I had to go off with her on my own. Like, no.

"I don't see what the problem is," said Pippa

now, sensing my embarrassment. "It's not like we have to sit around holding Hannah's hand all night, is it? There will be lots of other people at the party."

Ella looked hesitant, so I went for the kill.

"Pippa's right," I agreed. "And look at it this way—she'll probably get friendly with someone else and that will get her off our backs once and for all."

"We can hope, I suppose," said Ella. "It's not that we haven't tried to be nice to her; it's just that she's so . . ."

"Watch out—she's coming!" Christy nudged Ella in the ribs as Hannah pushed her way across the room toward us carrying a tray, with one bandaged thumb stuck in the air.

"Hi!" she said, flopping down on the one remaining chair. "Whew, it's hot. Don't you hate heat waves? Hey, I don't suppose any of you has any painkillers? Only, my thumb is throbbing like crazy."

"Oh, dear!" said Pippa in mock concern, leaning forward and inspecting the bandage at close quarters. "What on earth have you done?"

"It was a splinter," Hannah replied, holding the thumb out for inspection.

"I thought it was an amputation," muttered Ella.

It would seem that this was one of her more grouchy PMS days. Ella's lovely for three weeks out of every four, and pretty foul for the other one. We're used to it. It's best not to let it get to you.

"It was really deep and very sore," Hannah began, a frown puckering her forehead.

"What a shame!" Ella said with a gasp. "Are you sure you can make it to the party?"

"Don't be daft!" Hannah giggled. "It's not that bad."

"Pity," mouthed Ella to Christy. I caught Hannah's expression, and I could have sworn she noticed.

"Bad luck, Hannah!" Christy said quickly, clearly feeling as bad as me at Ella's grumpiness. "Why not get an aspirin from the office?"

"Okay, good idea. Hey, I've never been to a nightclub before," Hannah gabbled on eagerly.

"You wouldn't be going tomorrow if . . ."

I kicked Ella under the table. She smiled sweetly at me and continued unabashed.

". . . if it hadn't been for me!"

I let out a sigh of relief.

"She's right!" I butted in hastily, in the hope of putting an end to any more snide remarks. What she had said was true. When you have a mother like mine, wild nights out don't feature very highly on your social calendar.

"There will be plenty of time for all that sort of thing when you are older," Mum always says when I suggest anything remotely adult. Trouble is, I think by older she means about thirty-five.

But this time, I was in for a surprise . . .

"How would it be," Mum had asked one evening over supper, "if you and Ella shared a birthday treat? After all, her birthday is only two weeks after yours, and with all the problems they've got right now, I'm sure her parents won't feel like . . ."

Her voice trailed off as my father threw her a warning look.

"What problems?" I asked, although I might have known I was wasting my breath. That's the problem with having a father who's a vicar; you are supposed to love the whole of the human race, but never get to hear any of the juicy gossip. It's hugely frustrating.

"Nothing important," my mother had continued quickly. "Anyway, how about it?"

It was fine with me; Ella may be moody at times,

but she knows how to have fun and, to be honest, when I'm with her I feel like I'm quite a happening person as well. She's always been the coolest of the cool in our year, the sort of person everyone wants to get in with. This party would set the seal on my status in Year Nine.

At first, it had all gone really well. We drew up this list; Pippa and Christy were on it, of course, and Donna and Becky, and then we added ten others, all people we thought had a bit about them. And that's when the trouble started.

"That makes sixteen people!" my mother said in horror, when Ella and I shoved the list into her hand. "You can't take sixteen people bowling!"

"Bowling?" The disdain in Ella's voice sent shivers of alarm down my spine. "We're not going bowling."

"Really?" My mother's voice sounded calm enough, but I knew the telltale signs. Her neck was going pink. "I thought that was Tory's plan."

"It was just an idea!" I was desperate that Ella wouldn't think I lacked imagination. "We don't have to . . ."

"But, Tory," my mother interrupted, "you love bowling. You said that . . ."

"Bowling sucks!"

My mother's horrified expression checked me before I could say any more.

"Besides, it's Ella's day too," I continued hurriedly. "Maybe she's got a better idea."

"You bet I have!" Ella grinned. "The Landing Stage!"

My heart sank. Of all the things she could have suggested, that was the one guaranteed to give my mother apoplexy.

"The Landing Stage? That nightclub on the pier? Absolutely, categorically not! You're far too young to frequent places like that."

One of the good things about Ella is that she is a world expert on the manipulation of difficult parents.

"Oh, I know that normally it would be a no-no!" she said, giving my mother one of those brilliant smiles of hers. "But you see, they've just started having these new TA-RA-RA nights."

"These *what*?"

My mother is so yesterday at times, it's embarrassing.

"Teenage Rave and Ride-About Nights," Ella explained patiently. I actually saw my mother flinch at the word "rave," but Ella wasn't fazed.

"No one over seventeen is allowed in, there's no alcohol . . ."

"I should hope not!" my mother interjected.

". . . they have bouncers at the doors and you get free rides on the Ghost Train and the Hall of Horrors and Tower of Doom and everything and it ends at ten-thirty, which is fine, isn't it . . . ?"

My mother's eyes narrowed in the way they always do when she is trying to work out whether you are telling the truth, the whole truth, and nothing but the truth. Ella was ready for her.

"Look," she said, rifling around in her jeans pocket and producing a rather dog-eared luminous pink flyer, "this tells you all about it."

My mother scanned the leaflet and chewed her bottom lip. You could see she was desperate to find something wrong with the event—and was failing.

"Well, I don't know . . . you get such seedy types around the beach area and . . . what does your mother think?"

"Oh, Mum's very laid-back about it!" Ella declared. "She just wants me to have a good time—she's dead cool like that!"

Frankly, I thought that Ella's mum was so out of it these days that she wouldn't know what day of the week it was, never mind be clued-up about the local club scene. But, all credit to Ella, it was a clever move. My mother and Ella's mum are mates, and I knew full well that Mum wouldn't want to look like a stick-in-the-mud in front of Ginny.

"Well, I don't know," Mum murmured. "Five pounds a head will make it very expensive."

"Everyone can pay for themselves," Ella stressed. "That's what people do these days."

You have to explain the modern world to my mother in great detail. She's still stuck way back in the eighties.

"Well, in that case," she said, brightening considerably, "as long as we take you there, and fetch you . . . oh, all right, then!"

"Brilliant!" Ella cried, jumping up and down in her excitement. "And then, could we all come back here for something to eat and a sleepover?"

Now she really had gone too far.

"I'm not having sixteen people sleeping over and that is final!" my mother declared, wagging a finger at Ella. "We don't have the space, never mind feeding them all and . . ."

"But, Mum, the boys could double up and . . ." I protested.

"No way! If Danny moved in with Ben, neither of them would sleep and, of course, Leo is far too small to have his routine disrupted."

There are times when I wish someone had taught my parents about contraception. It was bad enough when it was just Danny, who's nine, and Ben, who's six, but then they went and had Leo, who is two and has the ability to reduce my mother to a gibbering idiot. It's always "the boys this" and "the boys that"—my social life, of course, is nothing to them.

"Well, what if everyone brings sleeping bags and we crash on the sitting-room floor or . . ."

"Tory!" My mother gave me The Look, which has been known to wither grown men at twenty paces. "I will settle for six, and that's my final word on the subject."

Even Ella knew when tactical withdrawal was the best move.

"Six is great," she said, smiling sweetly. "The rest can go home when the club night ends."

"That's settled then," my mother said smugly.

Ella turned to me.

"You, me, Pippa, Christy—and who else? Becky and . . ."

"Whatever," I said hastily, praying that my mother wouldn't start one of her "Is Becky the loud one with the stud in her eyebrow?" interrogations.

"You are such an angel, Mrs. Norris!" Ella enthused, giving my mum a hug. "Thanks so much!"

My mother, who thankfully succumbs very easily to flattery, merely smiled, patted Ella's hand affectionately, and disappeared into the kitchen.

Ella grinned and squeezed my arm.

"It's going to be so cool!" she whispered. "The Landing Stage is *the* place to go! You and I will be total stars!"

I heaved a silent sigh of relief. We were back on track, and everything was going to be fine.

Of course, that was before my mother stuck her nose in.

"You have invited Hannah to the party, of course?" she asked over breakfast on the Wednesday before my birthday.

"No," I replied, shaking my head. "She's not really our sort and . . ."

"Don't be so ridiculous!" my father interjected, spitting bits of muesli over the table in his indignation. "You hardly know the girl."

"Precisely!" I retaliated triumphantly. "So why would I want her at my party?"

"Because she's new to the area, she's had to start school in the middle of the year, and she doesn't know many people yet," Dad replied.

"And Angela's my friend," my mum added. "Think how it will look if you leave Hannah out."

"But . . ." I began. I might as well have saved my breath.

"Just remember how nervous you felt when we moved here, Tory," my father interrupted. "Put yourself in Hannah's shoes."

That's one of his catchphrases. I'm supposed to put myself in the place of starving Africans, screaming kids in Sunday School, and any number of old ladies who call me "Precious" and ask me the same question ten times each Sunday.

"Just be nice to her," my father concluded, as if that wasn't what we'd all been trying to do for weeks.

"I *am* being nice to her," I protested. "I positively ooze sweetness and light at school. But no way is she coming to the party, and that's final!"

Which of course it wasn't. My mother, whose deviousness is second only to her complete lack of social awareness, actually took it upon herself to write an invitation and stick it through Hannah's door.

That was why Hannah was now slurping her way through a can of Coke and babbling on about whether she should wear a skirt or jeans to the party.

"I've got some wicked new PJs for the sleepover," Christy began.

Hannah gasped. "A sleepover? Is there a sleepover too?"

"No—you remember, Christy, we canceled the sleepover!" I blurted out, glaring at her.

"We did? But I thought . . ."

"Because my mum's got visitors, and Tory's mum's got the kids to deal with," stressed Ella, catching on fast and jerking her head in Hannah's direction.

"Oh, right—yes!" Christy said, nodding. "I remember now."

I could see Hannah scanning our faces and, for a moment, felt really guilty. After all, we were her only friends, and she had helped me with my IT project the week before. I opened my mouth to speak—but then I caught the look of admiration that Ella was giving me and closed it again.

It was okay. Ella was happy, Hannah was happy, my mother had got her own way, and everything was on track for a brilliant party.

If I had known just how wrong I was, I wouldn't have felt quite so smug.

"They don't want me around, do they?"

Hannah's question, fired at me while we were filing into the classroom for afternoon registration, was so blunt that for a moment I was lost for words.

"Go on, admit it!" she urged, her dark eyebrows knitted together in a frown. "They just put up with me because I'm your friend!"

I swallowed hard and forced an expression of sheer amazement across my face.

"Of course they don't!" I assured her, feeling really guilty for having been so mean. "Whatever makes you think that?"

She sighed and chewed her bottom lip.

"I guess I'm just not their sort of person," she went on. "I do try to fit in—it's just that—well, what's happened this past year . . ."

For a moment, I thought she was going to burst

into tears on the spot, but she merely sniffed, pressed her lips together and gave me a wan smile.

"Sorry—stop looking back, that's what my mother says!" she blurted out. "She says we mustn't think about it, let alone speak of it. . . ."

"What?" I asked.

Hannah ignored me. "Of course, she would, wouldn't she? It's easy for her to forget, now that he's on the scene . . ."

Her voice trailed off as Mrs. Temple came striding into the room. "Settle down, 9T!" She thumped the register down on her desk and began reeling off names.

"Now *who's* on the scene?" I hissed at Hannah out of the side of my mouth.

"Toby," she replied curtly. "Although, if you ask me, Toyboy would be more apt." She spat the words out.

"What? You mean, your mother . . ." Mum hadn't said anything about this. Typical.

"Victoria Norris! Is it within the realms of possibility that you could stop talking and pay attention for more than ten seconds at a stretch?" Mrs. Temple banged her fist on the desk.

I waited until she had reached the end of the

register and started holding forth about the new library opening hours, and then turned back to Hannah.

"So this Toby is *who* exactly?"

Hannah sighed. "My mother's new man. She met him a couple of days after we moved down here. She's completely besotted. It's disgusting—he's tons younger than her, and so up himself!"

She nibbled her thumbnail.

"Since he came along, she's ignored me totally. It's all 'Toby' this and 'Toby' that."

"You've never said anything about him before," I whispered. "I thought it was just you and your mum."

Hannah shrugged. "If your mum was fawning all over some oily git, would you brag about it?"

She had a point, although the idea of my mother fawning over anyone stretched the imagination to its limits.

"I just keep hoping she'll get tired of him," Hannah went on. "Fat chance."

I opened my mouth to reply, but Mrs. Temple had just leaped to her feet.

"Victoria Norris, what have I just said?"

"The library will be open from eight-thirty every

morning except Wednesdays, and closed on Thursday lunchtimes, Miss!" I replied, giving her one of my butter-wouldn't-melt-in-my-mouth smiles.

Her face fell in disappointment.

"Right. Yes. Well . . ."

Clearly she didn't realize that by the time you are in Year Nine, you have cultivated the ability to listen to at least three conversations at once when absolutely necessary. From the other side of the room, Ella gave me a quick thumbs-up. Standing up to teachers always got you extra Brownie points from Ella.

"Right, 9T—to your classes now! Less talking, more action!"

She had her beady little eyes fixed on my face, so I waited until we were out of the classroom and halfway down the stairs before grabbing Hannah's arm.

"I knew your mum and dad had split up," I began, "but I didn't realize . . ."

"You don't know anything!" She whirled round and glared at me. "You don't have a clue, any of you!"

I was so stunned by her change of mood that I was lost for words.

"I'd like to see how you lot would cope with what I've been through this past few months! All the lies and the deceit and . . ."

Hannah broke off abruptly and stomped off down the stairs ahead of me, her immaculately cut jet-black hair swinging like one of those adverts for gloss-giving shampoo.

"I'm really sorry," I began, pushing past a couple of Year Tens to reach her. "I didn't mean . . ."

"That's what they all say—'I didn't mean it!' That's what Dad said when . . ."

Her voice trailed off and you could see that she had said more than she'd meant to.

"When what?" I urged her. I admit it—I was sorry for her, but I was dead intrigued as well.

"When he walked out! Not that it was all down to him. . . ."

Her voice cracked, and she turned away. "I don't want to talk about it, right?" She slung her school-bag over her shoulder, narrowly missing my right eye. "Mum's right—it's over. Just leave me alone!"

"But . . ."

I put a hand on her shoulder, and suddenly her mood switched again as she touched my arm.

"All I want is to start over, Tory—is that so bad?"

Hannah looked at me, her dark eyes pleading. "And I thought that with you and Ella and the others, it was going to be all right. I thought I could put my past behind me."

She looked so tragic that I felt like a real mean cow.

"I mean, what with your mum and my mum being friends . . ." she wheedled.

Perhaps my mum knew more than she had told me. It wouldn't be the first time. Perhaps we had all been horribly unfair.

"Of course it's all right!" I assured her, giving her arm a squeeze. "We're going to have a great time."

She smiled weakly.

"You're sure? Because now I'm going to be living across the road from you. . . ."

"What?" I hadn't intended to sound so alarmed. "I mean—really? How come?"

"Toby," she said. "He's given Mum a job at The Kittiwake."

"The Kittiwake? Are you serious?"

"Of course, why wouldn't I be?"

I gulped. We'd seen builders hammering away at The Kittiwake Hotel for months; Mum had read out the "Coming Soon" adverts in the local paper, saying that the refurbishment would turn it into the trendiest private hotel on the South Coast, and Dad had said he hoped they wouldn't have what he called a wretched thumping disco. Ella, Pippa, Christy, and I just wondered why anyone would want to come and stay in The Crescent.

All four of us lived on the same street. Even Donna and Becky, who were kind of in our gang and kind of not, lived in houses whose gardens backed onto The Crescent. It's a funny sort of road: posh houses with gravel drives at one end (where Ella lives), turn-of-the-century town houses with tiled steps and bay windows in the middle (where Christy and Pippa live) and a hotchpotch of modern boxes at the totally unfashionable east end, where I live. The irony of it is that Ella's house used to be the vicarage until the church decided to sell it off and make money and dump their vicars in a hideous 1970s monstrosity.

Living in The Crescent was how the four of us got together. When we started at Elmdean in Year Seven, most people had loads of mates—kids they'd been at primary school with. We weren't like that. Pippa had just come back from Singapore where her father had been doing something highly important for an oil company; I'd just moved to Westbeach from Eastbourne because Dad had got a new parish; and Christy had finally decided that being taught at home by her dotty half-Russian, half-Italian mother was more than she could stand. Which, if you'd met her mother, you'd fully appreciate.

And Ella? She'd been to some posh private prep school, which probably accounts for why she's a born leader. That's what she says, anyway. Some people say she's just plain bossy.

She certainly took charge on the day that Pippa and I moved in—the day the two removal vans blocked the street and Ella's father screamed at the drivers and almost had a punch-up because he couldn't get past in his silver Mercedes. She came belting up the road a few minutes later and apologized for her dad being so uncool.

She doesn't usually do apologies; that's probably why it sticks in my mind.

"What school are you going to?" she had demanded after my mother, doing her "Isn't it lovely for you to find new friends?" bit, had unearthed half a bottle of lemonade and some squashed digestive biscuits from one of the packing cases.

And when we had discovered that we were all headed for Elmdean, she announced that we'd stick together until we got the place sussed.

"It's destiny!" she assured us, halfway through her fourth biscuit. "I read my horoscope in Mum's paper this morning and it said that a tricky situation would be resolved by an encounter with new, like-minded people! And here you are!"

"What tricky situation?" Pippa asked.

"Well—your lorries blocking Dad's car, I guess!" she replied hastily.

"And how do you know we are like-minded?" Pippa asked. "We've only just met."

See what I mean? Dead logical, Pippa.

That's when Ella started checking out our star signs and going on about the sun being in the ascendant when we were born—or something like that. She's really good at it—she knows who is compatible with who and everything like that. I think it's all rubbish, personally, but I didn't let on. I was only thankful to have new mates. It's odd, but at my old school, when people heard that my dad had stopped being an IT manager to train to go into the Church, they started treating me differently—like I'd become some sort of goody-goody overnight. I thought Ella and Pippa might be the same.

"What? He's the new vicar? At St. Peter's?"

Ella had stared at me that day when I made the announcement.

"Yes, but it's okay. . . ."

"Brilliant, fantastic, ace, amazing!" She actually clapped her hands in excitement. "Brasses!"

"I beg your pardon?"

"They've got these amazing brasses in the crypt," Ella said. "I've been wanting to do rubbings for ages—I've got this brilliant idea for jewelery based on medieval figures you see and . . ."

That's when we discovered that Ella lives for art. Painting, sculpture, fashion design—you name it, she can do it. She says she's either going to be an interior designer or an illustrator or maybe an award-winning architect. At the time, though, I didn't care about all that; I was just so grateful not to have someone looking at me like I'd landed from another planet. My parents were dead chuffed too; Dad said she could have access to the crypt whenever she wanted if she came to church once a month. Very into bribery, my father.

It might have been just the three of us forevermore, except that on the first day of term, my mother reversed her car into a lamppost outside the school gates, which was humiliating in itself. What made it worse was that she managed to completely destroy the back end of a bicycle that was propped up against it.

"Oh, my goodness!" she'd cried, ramming on the handbrake and leaping out of the car. "Now look what you've made me do! You and your wretched music!"

Quite how Radio 1 could be responsible for my mother's total lack of concentration, I didn't know. What worried me more was that at least a dozen kids were gawping at the spectacle and at least half of them were laughing.

"My bicycle! My bicycle!" A vast woman dressed in purple cords and a velvet cape and sporting a huge felt hat had arrived, arms waving in distress. "Oh dear, oh dear, what has happened to it?"

"I told you not to leave it there, Mum!" An elfin-faced girl with a mass of auburn curls hanging round her shoulders had propped her own bike against the school railings and sighed deeply. "You never listen!"

I won't go into the details of my mother groveling and Christy's mother sobbing and my mother giving her a lift home and Christy spending the next two hours apologizing for her maternal parent and explaining that it was the Russian blood that made her so totally dotty. Suffice to say that by lunchtime on that first day, the four of us were rock-solid mates.

"My stars said that new relationships would be forged as the result of a catastrophe!" Ella had exclaimed. "And they have!"

And we've been friends ever since. Our parents are pretty friendly, too, which is all very well until you realize that they have this underground network going, through which they check up on everything we're doing. "Is it really true that there's no Maths homework this week?" "Are you honestly going to let Christy have highlights?" That sort of thing.

Of course, we do have other friends too, people like Becky and Donna who were in our set for ages until Becky fell in love and starting dating Warren, and Donna began chasing anything in trousers to keep up with Becky. But it was really just us four that mattered.

And then, in the summer term of Year Nine, Hannah came to Elmdean, and my mother thrust us together. To be fair, we did try to get friendly with her. Trouble was, Hannah never seemed to be happy doing the things we did. She hated going to the beach, but we put that down to the fact that she'd never lived by the sea and was scared of the water. But then we found that if we hung out down at the shopping center, she was only happy while she was spending money. As soon as she'd found what she wanted, she would complain that the piped music gave her a migraine. When we went to the cinema, she only wanted to see totally non-scary, boring kids' films and, when we played tennis, she sulked if she missed a ball.

So in the end, we just saw her at school, which was easy because she lived on the other side of town.

But now, if she was going to be on our very doorstep . . .

"But—you're not actually going to live at The Kittiwake, surely?" I asked, hoping that I might just have misheard.

Hannah nodded.

"Mum's going to be a sort of front-of-house person or something," she said. "Personally, I think it's just an excuse to live with The Creep!"

"But—surely the hotel must have cost a bomb!" I said.

Hannah nodded.

"It did—but then Toby's loaded, which is why my mother's latched on to him, of course."

I could tell from her tone of voice that she was not over-keen on her maternal parent.

"With her it's just money, money, money!" Hannah sighed and rubbed a hand across her eyes. "That's what made my dad—well, that's why he left."

I didn't know what to say.

"I thought that at least now I had you as a mate, things would be better, but if the others are going to be horrid to me . . ."

"The others will be just fine," I promised her. "You just need to . . ."

"To what?" Her eyes flashed.

I wanted to tell her to chill, to loosen up—but how could I? She was going through a tough time and parents can be so difficult. I should know.

". . . to get to know them better, that's all."

"I will," she said with a sudden grin. "You're great, you know that? Really great."

✳ 2 ✳
Parent Problems

"**Where are the others?**" I panted as I ran out of the school gate and caught up with Ella.

"Pippa's got tennis practice, Christy's rehearsing for the music festival, Donna's getting her highlights done for the party, and Becky's in detention. So you'll have to make do with me. Walk or bus?"

"Walk," I said. "It's too hot to sit on a bus. Besides, I need to talk to you. About Hannah."

"Oh puh-leese!" Ella sighed. "It's bad enough having to deal with her when she's hanging around, without having to talk about her when she's not here!"

"No, listen!" I insisted, making a big thing of looking over my shoulder to check that no one was listening. "I think you ought to hear this before any of the others."

That worked just the way I knew it would.

"Really? What?"

"There's something of a mystery going on

there," I began, as we crossed the road toward the park.

"Like what?"

"Well, you know that my mum said that Hannah's parents had split up?"

"So?" Ella was losing interest. "Loads of parents do that."

"I know, but Hannah was really upset earlier, and she said something about lies and deceit. Then she said that her dad had said he didn't mean any of it to happen."

"He didn't mean what to happen?" I had Ella's full attention now.

"I don't know, but I reckon he's done something awful—something that's scarred her for life!" Okay, so I'm good at drama. It's the only subject for which I always get A grades.

"What sort of awful?" said Ella, her eyes wide.

"I haven't found out yet, but take my word for it, it's serious."

I took a deep breath, held it, and starting biting my lip. That's what my drama teacher says you do to convey the idea that you are holding on to a big secret.

"Go on," urged Ella, pulling some lip balm from

her skirt pocket and ladling it onto her mouth. "There's more, isn't there?"

"Did you know that her mum is hanging out with a guy half her age?"

Okay, so I didn't exactly know the age difference, but it certainly had an effect on Ella.

"You mean—like—twenty-something?" Ella sounded incredulous.

I nodded.

"Thereabouts," I murmured vaguely.

"And they're living together?"

I shook my head.

"Not at the moment. Not until . . ."

Another pause.

"Until?"

"They've moved into The Kittiwake!"

Ella stopped dead in her tracks.

"The Kittiwake?" she gasped.

"Apparently," I gabbled on, "Toby the Toyboy has bought it and . . ."

Ella's pert features broke into a broad grin.

"That's neat!" she chuckled. "Toby—Toyboy. Good one, Tory!"

I didn't enlighten her that it wasn't my idea.

"So she's going to be living . . ." Ella's voice faded

at the enormity of what I had told her.

"On our street—yes," I finished. "But the thing is, Hannah hates this Toby guy, and she's obviously had some really awful things happen to her and, well, I know she's a dweeb, but don't you think we ought to try—just one more time—to be nice to her? At least until we know what happened?"

I waited for Ella to protest.

"You're right," she said eventually. "Actually—I feel pretty awful. I was really catty to her today. I didn't mean to—it just sort of came out. Time of the month, I guess."

"I was nasty too," I confessed, "and I don't even have that as an excuse. I mean, it was me who lied about us canceling the sleepover. Not that my mother would let us have . . ."

"We'll invite her!" Ella declared. "Ring her tonight and tell her."

"But we said the sleepover had been canceled," I began.

"Use your head, Tory!" she retorted. "Pretend your mother had a change of heart or something, okay? Then maybe we can find out what's going on."

"Great!" I knew she only wanted Hannah around so that she could be the one to find out the truth, but at least my conscience would be eased. Of course, if I'd asked anyone else, Mum would say enough was enough; but for Hannah, she'd bend all the rules.

"I reckon all Hannah wants is a fresh start— maybe now she's got it off her chest, she'll chill a bit!" I told Ella.

"Well, we need to find out what this business with her father is all about," Ella murmured. "But we have to be careful."

"You mean, be tactful and not ask too many questions?" I asked.

She shook her head.

"No, I mean there may be a jinx on her and we don't want it transferring to us and . . ."

I burst out laughing.

"Ella Foster, you are unreal!" I giggled. "There is no such thing as a jinx!"

"That," said Ella, "is a matter of opinion. You have to think laterally about these things."

I thought about those words quite a lot during the next couple of weeks.

It was just after tea. My father was practicing his sermon in front of the hall mirror, and I was hauling mattresses and floor cushions into my bedroom, ready for what my mother called "the forthcoming onslaught," while trying to stop Ben and Danny from playing SAS paratroopers on my bed, when Mum stormed into my bedroom.

"Boys! Downstairs! Now!"

"But . . ." began Ben.

"Before the count of three! One, two . . ."

Danny grabbed Ben's hand and they shot through the door. Even at their age, they know you don't mess with my mother when she's roused.

"What do you think you're doing?" she asked, hands on hips.

"Getting ready for the sleepover," I replied. "You told me to put . . ."

"Oh, the sleepover!" she repeated, her eyes flashing. "Would that be the sleepover that apparently I have just canceled?"

My stomach lurched.

"And don't try wriggling out of it, Victoria!" she stormed. It's always a bad sign when she uses my full name. "I've just had Hannah's mother on the phone!"

"But, Mum, we hadn't invited Hannah to the sleepover and . . ."

"So I discovered this morning when I had coffee with Angela!" she ranted on. "I said it must have just been an oversight and that, of course, Hannah must come and then you . . ."

"Mum! That is so not on!" I shouted, remembering Ella's words. "You can't tell me what to do. Besides, you said only six . . ."

"Naturally, I assumed Hannah would be one of the six," she stressed.

"You had no right to assume anything!" I shouted. "It's not your party."

"For as long as you live under this roof and your father and I pay the bills, young lady . . ." Mum began and then thought better of it. "Anyway, when Hannah got home from school, Angela told her about the sleepover. That's when Hannah said that you had told her it had been canceled."

She held my gaze. "The thing is, Hannah knew you were lying. She's not stupid."

I swallowed hard.

"Mum, let me explain," I gabbled. "Okay, so I pretended it was off. . . ."

"That was a barefaced lie!"

"Yes, but that was because Christy started talking about it, and I didn't want Hannah to feel left out."

I waited, hoping that my mother would appreciate my kindness. All she did was glare at me.

"But then Hannah told me what a terrible life she'd had this past year, and how she wanted a fresh start, and I felt awful so I had a chat with Ella and tried to persuade her to have Hannah after all."

"Oh, I might have guessed that Ella would be behind this somehow!" my mother said. "Can you actually breathe without Ella giving you permission, Tory?"

At least I was Tory again.

"It's not like that, Mum!" I retorted. "It is her party too, remember. Your idea."

My mother sighed and said nothing.

"Anyway, on the way home, me and Ella agreed that we were going to invite Hannah, but of course, I knew you'd said we could only have six sleeping over, and it would have been rude to ask someone else to drop out, so I was trying to think of a way of persuading you to let us have one extra."

It had been an effort, but I knew I had her. She didn't have a leg to stand on.

"Well, of course you can have her; I've already told Angela that we've got a spare sleeping bag."

She sighed.

"Poor Hannah—she knew something was going on and you're right—I get the impression things haven't been easy for them. Not that Angela talks about . . . anyway, I hope you will all do everything you can to make her feel at ease. It costs nothing to be nice to people, Tory."

"No, Mum," I said meekly and flung the floor cushion back in the corner of the room. "Sorry."

"We'll say no more about it," she agreed, ruffling my hair. "I guess you only lied to Hannah to save her feelings."

I think the pain in my chest was my conscience pricking.

I was just putting the finishing touches to my room, and was about to head downstairs for a milk shake, when I heard my mother's muffled tones wafting through the wall from her bedroom.

"Kay, is that you? Listen, the most amazing news!"

She was on the phone to Pippa's mum, which wasn't at all unusual. What was more interesting was that she was speaking in that kind of low half-whisper that parents use when they don't want to be overheard.

So, of course, I stopped pummeling duvets, opened my door slightly, and strained my ears.

"You know I would have told you before, but Angela made me promise not to breathe a word to a living soul until she gave me the all clear!"

This warranted the risk of stepping out on to the landing.

"Yes—yes, that's right! Yes, manageress—at The Kittiwake! Something about a business partnership."

And the rest, I thought, straining my ears to catch her words.

"Tell me about it! I know—Douglas reckons it must have cost an absolute fortune, but just think what it could mean for you and me!"

A pause while Pippa's mum obviously burbled on at the other end of the line.

"Well, the thing is, it could be the making of Breakwater Blooms! And it would help Angela too—having friends she could rely on not to let her down." The penny dropped. Pippa's mum and my mum set up this business last year, doing flower arrangements for weddings and parties and stuff. They've got this tiny studio at the bottom of Pippa's garden and they keep talking about expanding and getting a shop when they've made a name for themselves. Obviously supplying flowers to the hotel was part of my mother's business plan.

"Well, no, to be honest, she's a bit—you know, in your face, for me, but I can't help feeling sorry for her. It's hard moving to a new town . . . what?"

Another pause.

"Exactly! We owe it to her to help all we can."

The conversation was getting boring, and I was about to give up and get on with rearranging my bedroom when I heard my name.

"Well, exactly! Yes, Tory's a great buddy of Hannah's. . . ."

To think she tells *me* not to exaggerate.

"Pippa said what? Oh, nonsense—anyway, I get the impression that Angela's worried about Hannah settling in. Well, I know she's been there for nearly a term, but according to Angela, she's a very sensitive. . . ."

I strained to catch my mother's words over the bickering of Danny and Ben, who were playing Spider-Man on the staircase.

"And so, if we can make sure the girls take her on board, I reckon we'd have it in the bag. Yes, make a fuss of her, have her over . . . Oh, all right then, you get on—talk to you tomorrow, okay? Bye for now!"

I leaped back into my room as I heard the bed springs creak and my mother walk toward her bedroom door.

"Good heavens, Tory, it's going to be a frightful squash with all those people in your room," Mum said, sighing as she peered through my half-open bedroom door. "I don't see how you're going to get any sleep."

Like, hello? Did she really think sleep was top of our agenda?

"Perhaps seven people is too many, after all," I commented dryly.

"Boys! Keep the noise down, please. I can hardly hear myself think."

Mum turned back to me.

"Still," she said, deftly ignoring my remark, "you can drift downstairs if it gets too much, can't you?"

I followed her downstairs, squeezing past Ben, who was in the process of throttling Danny, and decided to go in for the kill.

"By the way, what happened to Hannah's dad?"

My mother frowned.

"I told you—the marriage broke up a year or so

ago," she said. "Anyway, it's not really any of our business. Angela never mentions her private life and neither should we, because . . ."

"So she didn't tell you she had a lover?"

"She has a . . . Tory, don't be so ridiculous!"

"What's a lover?" Ben stopped beating up Danny and looked inquiringly at Mum.

"Kissy-kissy yuk-yuk!" giggled Ben.

"You two—upstairs! Get ready for bed! Now!" my mother retorted, chasing them out of the room.

"But we've just come *down*stairs," Danny reasoned.

"Well, it will be good exercise for you to go up again, won't it?" Mum replied sweetly.

"Mothers!" Danny muttered.

He's a fast learner, my brother.

"Tory, you must watch what you say in front of the boys," my mother admonished. "All that nonsense about . . ."

"It's not nonsense," I protested. "Hannah says that her mother's seeing this guy. . . ."

"For goodness' sake!" my mother retorted. "Seeing someone is not the same as having a . . . well, being involved."

For someone with four kids, she's very uptight about sex, my mother.

"But Hannah said . . ."

"Angela is going into business," my mother stressed. "You might as well know, she's going to be helping to run . . ."

"The Kittiwake," I finished for her. "I know. Hannah told me."

"Yes, well, I have no doubt she will be seen around with half a dozen men over the next few weeks—that's the way these things work."

My mother made it sound as if her whole life was taken up with high-powered deals.

"Angela told me herself that she's finished with men," she added, and then bit her tongue as if she'd said too much. Honestly, it's amazing that a woman can reach the age of forty-three and be so naïve. I would have put her straight, only at that moment my mobile rang.

I pulled the phone from my jeans pocket and flipped open the cover.

"Hi, Tory! It's me, Hannah! Listen, I've been thinking—you're right."

"Who is it?" my mother hissed at me.

"Hannah," I mouthed.

"Be nice," she whispered back and disappeared into the kitchen.

"Tory, are you still there?"

"Yes—I was just about to phone you. Listen, about the party . . ."

"What? You don't want me there, is that it?" Her voice hardened.

"Don't be silly!" I replied, wishing she wasn't always so defensive. "It's just that—well, I'm really glad you're coming to the sleepover."

"Are you?"

Hannah didn't sound convinced.

"Yes," I retorted. "Look, I'm sorry—the only reason I said it was off was because Mum had made this big thing about us only having six people, and we'd invited them weeks ago, before we really knew you and . . ."

"That's okay!" To my relief she changed the subject. "Look, can I come over? Mum's at the hotel with The Creep, talking about light fittings or something and I'm bored brainless."

I knew it would be more than my life was worth to say no.

"That would be great," I told her. "Only Dad's got a meeting about to start and the boys are running riot all over the place. . . ."

"Wow, you're so lucky to have little brothers.

It's so lonely being an only child."

Personally, I would have thought a house free of damp nappies and small boys being Spider-Man all over the furniture would be sheer bliss.

"Feel free to borrow them at any time," I told her. "You get fined for returning them too early."

It wasn't that good a joke, but to hear the way Hannah laughed, you would have thought I had just won the Comedian of the Year award.

"You're so funny!" she chortled. "I wish I could think of funny things like that."

I knew she was just trying to be friendly but her gushiness was a bit sick-making.

"So—can I come over to the hotel instead?" I asked, thinking that I'd get to see this Toby and be one up on the others on the information front.

"I suppose," she said, sounding reluctant. "Only, the carpet fitters are crawling all over the place and Mum's in a foul mood. . . . Tell you what, we could go for a walk. I'll meet you outside your house in five minutes, okay?"

Foiled again.

"Fine," I agreed. "See you then."

I shoved my phone into my jeans pocket and pushed open the kitchen door, almost falling over

Danny's toy helicopter and half a dozen *Harry Potter* figures on the floor. Mum was mopping up the disgusting mess that always followed Leo's attempts to feed himself, and Leo was picking up squashed peas and sticking them up his nose.

"Tory, be a dear and take Leo upstairs and get him undressed," she asked. "I've got to finish . . ."

"Sorry, can't!" I told her, taking a step backward as Leo tried to wipe his hands all over my T-shirt. "I'm going out."

"Out?" My mother looked as astonished as if I'd said that I was going to enter a convent. "At this hour?"

"Mum," I replied, as patiently as I could. "It's half past seven. It's June—it's broad daylight. Believe it or not, people do venture outside, you know."

My mother pulled a face.

"You know what I mean," she said. "Where are you going?"

"To see Hannah," I admitted. "Her mum and the *boyfriend* . . ."

I put special emphasis on that word.

". . . are over at The Kittiwake and we're going for a walk."

"Oh, well then, that's absolutely fine!" Mum exclaimed, looking positively radiant at the idea. "Don't worry about the boys—I'll sort them once the Pastoral Committee lot have arrived. You go and have fun!"

I grabbed my shades from my bag. Sunshine always makes me sneeze. So uncool.

"And if you see Angela, give her my love! Tell her to pop in for a coffee if she feels like it."

"Should I give her the phone number of Breakwater Blooms while I'm at it?"

For once, my mother was at a loss for words. I took advantage of this rare event and sped down the hall and out of the front door before she could draw breath.

I saw Hannah crossing the road toward me, and she wasn't alone. Her mother was with her.

"There you are, Victoria!" Mrs. Soper pecked my cheek and a great waft of perfume assailed my nostrils.

"She likes to be called Tory," Hannah interjected firmly.

"Oh, surely not—not with a lovely, regal name like Victoria!" Mrs. Soper cried.

Hannah and I exchanged glances, and she mouthed "Sorry!" at me. As one who has to apologize for my mother's behavior on a regular basis, I could sympathize.

"All ready for tomorrow night?" Mrs. Soper leaned toward me, and her tone changed abruptly.

"Yes," I gulped, trying to stifle a sneeze at the second onslaught of perfume. "Did my mum tell you we've got a spare sleeping bag, Hannah?"

I have always believed that you need to keep the upper hand in tricky situations.

"She did indeed." Mrs. Soper nodded, as Hannah opened her mouth and shut it again. "And Hannah's really looking forward to it, aren't you, poppet?"

She didn't wait for poppet to reply, but burbled on.

"So we'll say no more about the silly little mix-up," she announced, holding my gaze. "All friends together, that's what I say!"

I grinned broadly, not so much from relief that she wasn't going to make a scene, as in the hope that she would think I was over the moon about the party, when in fact it was her appearance that had me in hysterics. We used to think Christy's mum (who dresses in velvet from head to toe and always wears a hat, even when she's cooking supper) was a bit bizarre, but we put that down to her being half-Russian; I was wondering just what excuse Hannah's mum had. She was wearing the tightest pair of leopard-skin trousers I have ever seen, diamanté stiletto sandals, and a gold Lurex top with the sort of plunge neckline that makes you want to look anywhere but at her chest. I couldn't believe that she and my mother were friends; Mum's style is much more "department store meets charity shop."

"Hannah's a sensitive girl who takes things to heart and . . ."

"Mum!" Hannah's cheeks were bright red, and I felt for her even more. "Shut up, will you?"

She grabbed my arm and began walking as fast as possible down the road.

"Bye!" trilled her mother. "See you later! Miss you already!"

"Sorry about my mother," Hannah said with a sigh, not slackening her pace until she saw Mrs. Soper crossing the road and entering the hotel. "She can be such a pain."

"All mothers can," I assured her. "I think they

teach them how to be difficult as part of their prenatal classes!"

We crossed the road and cut down Princes Avenue to the seafront.

"Ice cream?" Hannah said, waving a ten-pound note in my face.

"Wow! Yes, please!"

"Look," she said, queuing up at the mobile van that always sat by the Krazy Golf. "Can I ask you something—as my best mate?"

"Of course," I said, slightly worried at the new role she had cast for me.

"You've been really nice to me, asking me to the sleepover and everything—but what can I do to make the others like me?"

"What do you mean?" I asked, only half concentrating while I deliberated on the merits of a Chocowhirl over a strawberry sundae.

"Well, I keep trying to be friendly, but it doesn't seem to work." She sighed. "I mean—take Christy. She's hardly said two words to me all term. So where am I going wrong?"

I grinned.

"Oh, don't worry about Christy; she's like that," I explained. "She's really dreamy—she composes music in her head and there's not much room for anything else. She's not a great talker—lives in a world of her own!"

Hannah looked doubtful.

"She ignores me half the time as well," I added to make her feel better.

"So you think she likes me okay?"

"Christy gets on with almost everyone," I replied, silently patting myself on the back for my tact.

"Ella doesn't though, does she?" Hannah snapped back, as we reached the head of the queue. "A Chocowhirl and . . . what are you having?"

"Same, please!"

Hannah handed over the money and thrust a cone in my hand.

"I get the feeling that Ella just doesn't want me around."

"Oh, Ella's just . . . Ella!" I said feebly. "She can come across as bossy at times, but that's just because she's an action person. She likes people to be feisty, I guess—she doesn't have much time for wimps."

"And you all think I'm a wimp." It wasn't a question. Her eyes were moist already, and suddenly I felt really guilty.

"Of course not!" I told her, fixing a bright smile on my face and kicking myself for being so stupid. "I'm just saying—she likes to have fun and take risks and if you want to be her mate, it's best to be spunky. Have a laugh, you know?"

I paused, licking my ice cream.

"Actually, I think she's got awful problems at home right now—something my mother said, but don't say I said so."

"Of course I won't," Hannah said, smiling for the first time.

"Shall we go and walk on the beach?" I suggested, in the hope that she would stop her interrogation.

Hannah gave a little shudder and shook her head.

"All those pebbles," she said. "I only like sandy beaches."

I counted to ten and managed to hold my tongue.

"And Becky? She's got a boyfriend, yes?" Hannah asked, wiping ice cream from her chin. "The guy who meets her from school?"

"Boyfriends plural!" I grinned. "She manages to fall in love about three times a week!"

Hannah nodded slowly as if memorizing a spelling list.

"She and Donna are both boy crazy," I added. "I guess that's why we don't see so much of them these days—they spend every break-time hanging around the school gates to ogle the guys from St. Edmund's!"

Hannah sighed. "I've never had a boyfriend. Have you?"

I shook my head.

"Not much chance at an all-girls comprehensive, is there?" I said. "Not that it bothers me. Boys are so—loud."

No way did I want her to know that actually, now that I was within a day of being fourteen, I was a bit worried about my lack of sex appeal. My boobs are so small they look like tacks, and when a guy does chat to me, I get all flustered and go pink. Ella says that I should just pretend I'm acting in some sultry movie. Trouble is, I don't think my face does sultry very well.

"Talking of boyfriends," Hannah interjected, breaking in on my thoughts, "I guess we'd better start back—The Creep's taking us out to supper at Scrummies."

"Wow! Lucky you!"

"Lucky? Hardly. Watching those two going all dewy-eyed over each other—it's enough to turn your stomach."

I thought to myself that I'd watch open-heart surgery if it meant a free meal at the best restaurant in town.

"I like Pippa best," she blurted out, just as I thought I'd managed to change the subject. "Next to you, of course. She's your best mate, right?"

Hannah's wide eyes were glued to my face.

"I'm friends with them all, really—but yes, I guess so," I shrugged. "Not that we're anything like one another—she's dead sporty and brilliant at Science and Maths, and I can't even catch a ball or add up! I love drama and English, and she thinks Jane Austen is a make of sports shoe!"

She giggled.

"I'd love to be like you lot," she said, sighing.

"Just be yourself," I replied, which was pretty alarming because it meant I had done what I always vowed I would never do—sound like my mother.

"What should I wear tomorrow?" Hannah asked as we emerged from the alley into The Crescent.

"Whatever you want," I told her. "Jeans, dress, whatever."

"Oh gosh, I haven't got a clue. . . ."

"Hannah, it's no big deal! Do your own thing, okay?" My patience was rapidly running out.

She beamed at me and looked genuinely happy for the first time in ages.

"I will," she said. "I promise!"

* 3 *
Pier Pressure

Ella danced toward me. "It's going okay, isn't it?" she shouted above the disco.

I nodded. "Great!" I said, striking a pose as the DJ faded out the latest SugaClub 4 hit. "Whew, I'm hot—must grab a drink before I expire."

Ella followed me to the juice bar.

"Hannah seems to be having a ball," she observed, gesturing across the crowded room to where Hannah was chatting to Becky, Donna, Laura, and Mel. "I've never seen her so bubbly."

"I said she might latch on to someone else, didn't I?" I remarked.

"But that lot?" Ella laughed. "I would have thought they were poles apart."

"Drink?" The guy behind the bar tapped on the counter.

"Oh, a banana smoothie please," Ella said.

"Make that two," I added.

"I have to admit," Ella went on, "it was a cool

idea of Hannah's to bring her camera, wasn't it? A real ice-breaker."

Hannah had been snapping away all evening while we danced, even standing on tables to get the best shot until the disco manager told her off.

"And what about those presents she bought us?" I added. "They were amazing."

"I've seen those necklaces in Funkyfings," Ella agreed, fingering the choker she'd put on the moment Hannah had given it to her. "They cost a bomb!"

She sighed.

"It makes me feel awful about the naff present I gave you," she admitted. "I mean, you're my best mate, but it's just that . . ."

Ella's voice trailed off and I could see that she was really embarrassed.

"Don't be silly!" I told her, glowing inside at her remark. "What's naff about hair mascara? Do I or do I not look a million dollars?"

Ella grinned.

"Besides," I assured her, "It's not like she saved up—when I told Hannah that she shouldn't have spent so much on my earrings, she'd just said that she'd got her mum to top up her allowance.

Apparently, she paid for Hannah's outfit without a murmur."

Hannah had stunned us all by turning up in black satin trousers, a sequinned halter-neck top, and the most amazing embroidered strappy sandals. To be honest, I began to feel that even the low-rise trousers and vest top that Mum and Dad had given me for my birthday were boring compared to Hannah's clothes.

"Lucky her!" Ella retorted. "She doesn't know she's born. She should try living . . ."

She stopped abruptly as the DJ flashed the strobe lights.

"Okay now, babes and boys!" he cried. "We've raved, so now we . . ."

He paused and threw up his arms, waiting for the crowd to respond.

"Ride About!" we all yelled.

"You've got it," he drawled. "All rides on the pier totally free—half-price grub at the food stalls and Gary down at the dodgems on the esplanade is flinging in four rides for the price of two—so go have a ball!"

"What first?" Pippa panted up to us with Christy close behind. "Ghost Train?"

"No, Tower of Doom," urged Ella.

"Okay then, so Ghost Train, Tower of Doom, Helter-skelter, then the Psychospin . . ." Pippa gabbled.

Christy sighed. "Pippa, hang on—let's just go with the flow, okay?"

"Yes, but if we don't plan . . ." Pippa insisted.

"Let's see what the others are doing," I suggested hastily, as we pushed our way through the cluster of kids spilling out into the fresh air.

We caught up with Becky and her mates, but there was no sign of Hannah.

"Which ride do you fancy?" I asked Becky, anxious to get ahead of the rush.

"What do you care? You won't want to be on the same ride as me, will you?"

"What . . . ?" I began.

"Mind you," snarled Donna. "The feeling is mutual!"

"Hang on," I began, but they were already flouncing off down the pier with Laura and Mel.

"What was all that about?" I gasped.

Ella shrugged. "Don't ask me," she said, dragging me toward the Tower of Doom. "Unless she's jealous because of the way that guy was all over you earlier."

"Tory had a guy?" Christy made it sound about as unlikely as my winning the World Chess Championships.

"You must have noticed," Pippa replied. "The poor lad was clearly besotted."

I felt myself blush and turned to look out to sea.

"He wasn't!" I protested, as the queue shuffled slowly forward. "Anyway, I know him vaguely. He used to go to my old drama club and we just got chatting. . . ."

"*We just got chatting!*" Ella teased. "And dancing and laughing, and fluttering the eyelashes. . . ."

"That is so not true!" I dug her in the ribs. "He danced with loads of people—oh!"

"Oh, what?" Pippa asked.

"Well, he'd been dancing with Becky—you don't think she fancied him and reckons I muscled in, do you?"

"That will be it." Christy nodded. "You know what she's like when it comes to . . ."

Her musings were interrupted by peals of laughter resounding all around us.

"Tory! Ella! Help!"

We turned and there was Hannah, one heel stuck firmly in between the slatted decking of the pier. She looked so funny that we all burst out laughing.

"I can't move," she whimpered

"Well," spluttered Ella, "if she will dress for the catwalk, what does she expect?"

"Just take them off and go barefoot," I called out to Hannah.

"They're all scratched now," she wailed, catching up with us and hitching her camera strap over her shoulder, "and they cost a fortune."

"That's why we wore flatties," Pippa explained patiently.

"You should have said," Hannah retorted, turning to me. "You never said anything about not wearing heels."

"Hannah, it's a pier," Ella said, butting in. "Have you never been on a pier before?"

"No," Hannah snapped. "They don't have piers in the middle of Birmingham." She looked at her ripped heels mournfully. "I'm going to look a real dweeb now," she moaned.

"It's fine," I butted in hastily before she could burst into tears. "No one is going to notice. Come on, we're going on the ride."

Hannah looked upward, her eyes popping out of

her head as she saw the height of the tower.

"What do you have to do?" she asked nervously.

"You don't *do* anything," Pippa explained, pushing her ahead up the steps. "You get in this cage thing, and it drops down halfway, then it lurches back up and then down again a bit farther. . . ."

"And the best bit is," added Ella, "that you don't know when the final drop is coming—that's the stomach-churning bit."

"And it's pitch dark," Christy added with a mock shudder.

"I don't know. . . ." Hannah began.

"It's great, honestly," I assured her. "You'll love it."

It took ages to get to the top of the stairs, but we were almost there when Hannah grabbed my arm.

"I can't do it!" she gabbled. "Honestly, Tory, I can't."

I turned. Her face was as white as a sheet, and she was actually shaking.

"Don't be silly!" Ella said sternly. "You've got to do it now—you can't go all the way back down."

"I can! I will, I have to!" Hannah actually burst into tears. "Come with me, Tory—please."

"Tory can't miss her go because of you," Pippa retorted. "Go down on your own if you must."

"Move along there!" The ride attendant was rapidly losing patience.

"If you're scared, just think of something else until it's over," Christy said, nudging Hannah forward. "That's what I do."

Hannah shook her head.

"It won't work," she stammered. "You have to come with me, Tory. Please. I'll throw up if I stay up here any longer."

"Okay," I said, because people were beginning to snigger and stare. "You go first, I'll follow."

She clutched the handrail and began tentatively to ease her way down.

"And you thought that the party would be a chance to get her off our backs?" Ella hissed at me. "Dream on!"

It was when we were halfway down that I saw Alex, the guy I'd been dancing with, clambering up with a bunch of his mates.

"Chicken!" one of them called.

"You're not backing out?" Alex sounded disbelieving. "You said you loved scary rides."

"I do—it's my friend, she's . . ."

"Oh, yeah, yeah," chorused the other guys. "Sure it is."

I just managed to resist the urge to shove Hannah all the way down those wretched steps.

"I'm sorry. I'm fine now."

Hannah rubbed a hand across her brow and smiled at me apologetically.

I didn't feel in the mood to smile back.

"That was really kind of you," she said. "I don't know why Pippa says you're difficult. I think you are the easiest person on earth to like."

My heart missed a beat.

"Pippa said that?"

Hannah nodded.

"Compared with Ella, she said. But don't worry—I'm sure she didn't mean it."

She slipped her arm through mine.

"Look, here come the others!"

"That was so cool," Ella said with a wide grin.

"Do you want to come up again with me, Tory?" Pippa asked. "You know, because you missed your turn."

I shook my head. I was still smarting from Hannah's remarks. I couldn't believe Pippa had said that I was difficult—it was always me who was bending over backward to make sure that the rest of them were happy.

"Fancy coming on the Ghost Train?"

There was a tap on my shoulder. I wheeled round to see Alex and his mates, Coke cans in their hands, grinning at us.

"Or will you be too scared?" asked the tall one with the unruly hair.

That did it.

"As if!" I retorted. "Nothing scares us."

"Too right," Ella added. "Let's go."

Alex introduced his mates as Rob and Steven and we began piling into the cars. Alex and Rob went in with me and Christy, and Ella winked and slipped into the one behind with Steven and Pippa. Hannah tried to climb in next to me, but Ella grabbed her arm.

"Come with us, Hannah," she urged. "Since you're the one who gets frightened easily."

It was one scary ride. I mean, I know it's all special effects and audio animatronics and stuff, but the bit where the severed head falls into your lap was so lifelike that I screamed and grabbed Alex's hand. Of course, I was dead embarrassed and tried to snatch it away, but he held on all through the ride and only let go a few seconds before we emerged into the fading daylight.

"So?" Pippa whispered in my ear. "What happened?"

"Nothing," I said and walked on. If she thought I was going to confide in her after what she had said about me to Hannah, she was wrong.

We went on a couple more rides and bought a whole load of candyfloss and toffee apples and mucked around in the Hall of Horrors, making stupid faces and behaving like little kids. Becky and Donna were in there too, but every time I tried to catch Becky's eye, she turned away. I was beginning to feel quite down about it all, when Steven had his idea.

"Let's have a dodgem crash-bash," he cried.

"A what?" Christy looked bemused.

"Don't mind Steve," Alex said, grinning. "He doesn't speak the same language as the rest of humanity. Dodgem cars—down on the esplanade?"

"Ace!" Ella clapped her hands. "I'm evil behind the wheel."

"Wow—wouldn't that make a brilliant one?" Christy said, gazing into the middle distance.

We stared at her.

"Wouldn't what make a brilliant what?" demanded Ella.

"Dance routine," Christy said. "Give the dancers steering wheels and have dodgem cars in the background and the music would have to be really vibrant and discordant to represent the speed and then—"

I put my hand across Christy's mouth and grinned at Alex.

"And you think *Steve* speaks a foreign language?"

Everyone laughed.

"Don't mind Christy," Pippa added. "She's artistic."

Christy grinned good-naturedly.

"When I'm a famous choreographer . . ."

". . . or composer," chipped in Ella. We'd had this conversation a dozen times before.

". . . you'll be sorry you mocked me. Last one to the dodgems is a weed!"

We all belted down the pier to the turnstile to get our hands stamped for re-entry.

"Tory," Hannah began, pushing between Alex and me and nudging my arm. "I thought your mum said we had to stay on the pier."

Have you ever had times when you wanted to put your hands round someone's throat and squeeze tightly? If so, you'll know how I felt. I could sense Alex staring at me in disbelief. Of course, Hannah was right—but then my mother says a lot of things that you just have to nod and say yes to, and then quietly forget about.

"I don't want you leaving the pier," she had told us sternly when she dropped us off. "You get all sorts of unsavory types on the seafront on a Saturday night."

She had glanced 'round as if half expecting a riot to break out behind her.

"We won't, Mrs. Norris," Hannah had simpered. "Promise."

Well, she could promise all she liked but I was going with the others. I mean, for heaven's sake; the dodgems were only about five hundred meters from the pier, there were floodlights all around, and the whole area was packed with people. I was hardly going to be abducted.

"So we'd better not go, right?" Hannah persisted, lingering by the turnstile.

Alex had already begun to go ahead with the others, and suddenly I knew that, no matter how much Hannah whined, I wasn't going to be taken in this time.

"So you stay," I snapped. "Do what you like—I don't care. It's my party and I'm going to have fun."

I pushed through the turnstile without a backward glance.

We had a brilliant time. It was a riot—Ella and Rob went in one car, Steven and Christy in another, and me and Alex in the third.

"Who's Pippa going with?" Christy asked anxiously. "Where's Hannah?"

"Whining," I muttered.

"I'll go on my own and then we can swap 'round," Pippa suggested cheerfully.

"Are you sure?" I asked, forgetting for a moment that I wasn't speaking to her. "I don't mind. . . ."

"Get in the car," Pippa ordered. "Since it's perfectly obvious that I shall be the most skillful driver, it makes sense for me to go it alone."

By the time we had all had several rides, I found myself feeling guilty about leaving Hannah behind. I had assumed she would follow us in the end, but there was no sign of her. I knew we ought to go and find her, but I didn't want to be the party pooper and break up the fun. I edged away from the dodgems, craning my neck in the hope of spotting Hannah.

"Where are you going?" Ella asked.

"I suppose I'd better check that Hannah is okay," I told her. "Remember what I told you about her mother making a scene?"

"I'll go," Ella replied decisively. "I need the loo anyway."

"Okay, then, and we'll pick up some chips on the way back," Pippa added. "I'm starving."

"No vinegar on mine!" Ella called as she ran off. "See you in ten minutes."

"Seven!" Pippa shouted back. "Otherwise the chips will be cold."

She's so precise.

We had only just got our cones of chips when the voice of the DJ wafted down from the pier over the loudspeaker system.

"Half an hour to go and counting! Let's shake to the sounds of Spiky Haircuts!"

"They're my fave band," Christy cried. "Come on!"

The boys loitered about kicking cola cans and doing the dumb things boys do when they are hyper, but we all ran back to the pier and into the club.

"Have you seen Ella?" Pippa shouted at me from

the door. "I've got her chips and they won't let me bring food inside."

"She's gone to the loo." Hannah appeared at my left elbow. "Give them to me and I'll take them over to her.

She grabbed them from Pippa and scuttled off across the pier in the direction of the ladies' loos.

"She's not so bad, I guess," Pippa remarked, turning to me. "She could be worse."

"Oh, sure she could," I snapped. "She could be as difficult as me, couldn't she?"

"What?" Pippa frowned.

"Forget it!" No way was I going to spoil the party by having a slanging match with Pippa. "I'm going to dance."

I joined Christy and Laura and a crowd of others on the dance floor and bopped for ages. Then Hannah joined in, strutting her stuff and laughing and joking with everyone. It was as if she had suddenly learned how to chill.

"Where's your friend?" Alex appeared through the crowd and touched my arm.

"Which one?" I asked, still dancing.

"Helen? Ellen?"

"Oh, Ella," I corrected him. "Come to think of

it, I don't know. Haven't seen her for ages. Why?"

"Steve fancies her," Alex said, grinning. "I think he wants to ask her out."

"Really?" I gulped.

He nodded.

"What's so odd about that?"

"Nothing," I replied hastily, as though we all got invited out by guys every day of the week. "I'll see if I can find her."

I pushed my way through the crowd and out on to the pier. It took a moment for my eyes to grow accustomed to the fading light, but then I spotted her. She was leaning over the railing and looking out to sea.

"Hey, Ella, guess what? That guy Steve wants to ask you out and . . ."

I touched her shoulder but she merely shrugged me off.

"Come on, you're going to miss the last dance and he's probably waiting for . . ."

"Like I care."

She looked up and I could see at once that she had been crying.

"Ella, what's wrong?" I gasped. Ella never cries— she says tears are for wimps and that sobbing damages your aura.

She turned away.

"As if you cared," she mumbled.

"Of course I care—you're my mate!" I insisted.

"Oh, really? And do you go blabbing to Hannah about all your mates, making up stories and . . ."

"What the hell are you on about?" I said in disbelief. "I haven't . . ."

"You told Hannah that I was a bossy cow!" she said, choking on the words. "And you . . ."

"I didn't!" I exclaimed.

"Oh, really?" Ella spun round to face me. "And I suppose you didn't tell her that my parents lives are a total mess either?"

"No way!" I was almost sobbing myself by now. "Ella, you know I wouldn't talk about you like that. I know what it feels like—it's bad enough that Pippa . . ."

I stopped.

"What about Pippa? Been telling lies about her too, have you?"

"Stop it!" I shouted. "Pippa told Hannah that I was a difficult person. I mean, it's bad enough that she thinks that, but to tell Hannah of all people . . ."

"Pippa said that?" Ella's eyes widened. "Pippa's never nasty about anyone."

"Well, she is now," I retorted. "I'm so much more difficult than you, apparently."

Ella gave the faintest smile.

"True," she nodded.

"You . . ."

"Just joking, silly."

Ella grabbed my arm and looked at me intently.

"Hang on—let's think this through."

She leaned back against the railing and frowned.

"What about the things you said to Hannah about Becky and Donna?"

"What things?" This was getting ridiculous.

"Becky told me just now—you said Donna and Becky were . . ."

She paused.

"Were what?"

"Slags," she said.

I was incandescent.

"I wouldn't even use that word, and besides I never, ever . . . oh, my God!"

Ella eyed me warily.

"What?"

"*Just ten more minutes, boys and babes—last drinks now!*" The loudspeaker blared above our heads. We both ignored it.

"Yesterday," I breathed. "The two-faced, manip-ulative little . . ."

"What about yesterday?" Ella urged.

"Hannah wanted to go for a walk, right? And it was just after all that business with my mum and the sleepover, so I thought I ought to go."

"And?"

"Hannah started pumping me for information about you and Pippa and Christy," I went on.

"So you *did* tell her those things!" Ella wheeled away and turned her back on me. "And I thought you . . ."

"NO! Listen," I urged her, as the music pumped out from the disco. "She was moaning on about wanting to make friends, and she kept saying that Christy ignored her and I told her that Christy lived in a dreamworld and ignored all of us half the time—and then she asked about Becky and Donna and . . ."

I was falling over my words in my haste to put the record straight.

"What did you say?"

"I said that they were boy crazy," I admitted. "I joked about the way they eye up the boys from St. Edmund's. But I never called them . . ."

"Okay, okay," Ella interrupted. "And what about me? What did you say about me?"

I took a deep breath. I knew that at this point, only the truth would work.

"I said you liked people to be spunky and feisty, and if she wanted to be your mate, perhaps she should chill out a bit," I admitted.

"Hannah said you called me a bossy cow!"

"I didn't—I did say that you could seem bossy at times. . . ."

"Oh great! Thank you for nothing."

"Ella, listen—what I meant was, that you are a born leader; you see what needs to be done and you're usually right."

She said nothing but looked a bit calmer.

"And then," I went on, "because she kept on about how you weren't nice to her, I said that my mum had mentioned that you had a few problems at home. . . ."

"Your mother said that?" Even in the twilight, I could see that Ella's face was flushed.

"Only to explain why she wanted you to share my birthday treat," I went on, praying that I was saying the right thing. "She'd only half-said it when my dad shut her up. She wouldn't say any more."

"So who else have you babbled to about my private life?" Ella was almost in tears again.

"No one," I assured her. "I haven't breathed a word to anyone else. I swear it on the Bible."

Ella chewed her lip.

"I guess you haven't then," she said. "You'd never swear like that if you had."

She paused.

"It's true, actually," she said softly. "My dad's business has gone down the pan. He's lost loads of money."

"I'm really sorry," I said, touching her arm. "My mum never told me that."

"My mum's in an awful state—she's not eating and she keeps shouting at everyone," Ella mumbled. "And she looks like death warmed up."

"That's awful," I began, realizing at once why my parents wanted me to share the party. "I didn't . . ."

"Don't let's talk about it—not now," she interrupted. "And don't you dare breathe a word to a living soul, because if you do, I'll never, ever speak to you again."

"I won't, I promise," I assured her.

"Now, listen," she went on, brightening suddenly. "I've got an idea."

I knew she would feel better taking charge, so I waited for her to carry on.

"It's clear that Hannah's trying to make trouble. I bet Pippa never said that about you . . ."

"I hope not," I muttered fervently.

". . . so we are going to find out once and for all. I'll tell Pippa and Becky what's going on, okay? You just keep Hannah busy and pretend nothing's happened. When we get home, just act normal and friendly."

I gasped. "What? And let her get away with it?"

"Oh, no." Ella smiled wryly. "Getting away with it is the last thing Miss Hannah Soper is going to do. Now, what were you saying about Steven?"

* 4 *
Pillow Talk

"Okay, so who's going first?" Ella waved my copy of *Heaven Sent* in the air. "Pippa—you're Sagittarius, right?"

Pippa pulled her sleeping bag up round her neck and nodded, trying not to look as if she knew the plan.

Ella started reading. "'You'll have a good week as long as you manage to steer clear of mates who enjoy spreading gossip about you. Someone is out to do you down so don't believe all you hear.'"

I shot a sideways glance at Hannah, but she was sitting on the end of my bed, hugging her knees and looking really interested.

"Okay, Becky," Ella went on. "Pisces, yes?"

"Aries," Becky corrected her. "Do you really believe in all that stuff?"

I had to stifle a smile. She had delivered her line perfectly.

"Judge for yourself." Ella shrugged. "Right,

where is it? Oh, yes. Here we are."

She peered at the page. "'This is a week for socializing, but be on your guard. It is dangerous to believe everything you are told, especially now that someone is going to try to break a friendship with idle gossip.'"

Ella looked up.

"Ring any bells?"

Becky shrugged.

"No, it's all a load of . . . oh! Well, I mean . . ."

She glanced at Hannah. Hannah was examining her toenails.

"What?" urged Ella. "I mean, be fair—you say it's rubbish, but if it means something, you ought to admit it."

"Well," Becky began, and I had to admire her timing. "It's just that—someone did say something to me tonight. . . ."

"Go on," Ella encouraged her. "Who?"

Becky wriggled on her floor cushion and looked at Hannah again. Hannah had moved on to nibbling her thumbnail and inspecting the pattern on the duvet cover.

"I don't want to say, really," Becky said innocently. "I hate gossip."

Christy almost gave the game away by spluttering into her hand, but you couldn't blame her. Becky was usually the first person in the entire year to babble any gossip she heard.

"Read mine, then," I begged Ella, right on cue. "Gemini."

"'This is a week for celebrating. . . .' Well, that's right, isn't it? Your birthday and everything. . . ."

"Get on with it!" Pippa interrupted, and I knew she was having a tough job keeping a straight face.

"'. . . but unless you deal with a spiteful enemy, it could all end in tears. Let them know that you're no fool and sort it out before it's too late.'"

We all glanced toward Hannah. Her face was slightly pink but, apart from that, she seemed unfazed.

"Do mine!" she said brightly, sliding under her duvet. "I'm Capricorn."

"I know," Ella said, and you could tell her mind was racing. We had expected her to crack before now. "Okay, here we are. Ready?"

Hannah nodded.

"'Don't take friendships for granted this week. Before you tell any more lies, think about what you would feel like if someone lied to you. If you carry on as you are, you will find yourself deserted by everyone. . . .'"

We could tell that Ella was improvising as fast as she could.

"'. . . you wanted to be close to . . .'"

"Shut up! Shut up!"

Hannah had clamped her hands over her ears and hunched her shoulders. Ella gave us a quick thumbs-up.

"What's wrong, Hannah?" Donna asked innocently.

Hannah looked up. She was on the verge of tears. Christy and I exchanged looks and I knew we were both feeling just a little bit guilty.

"Sorry," Hannah said quickly. "It's just that . . . it's so spooky. I mean, I never believed in horoscopes and stuff like that before, but what you just said—it's all happened."

"It has?" Ella gave what she clearly thought was a sympathetic look. "How do you mean?"

"My dad," Hannah said flatly. "He's deserted me."

We looked at her in stunned silence. This wasn't part of the plan.

"He lied to me too."

I looked at Ella and shook my head slightly. She

stuffed the magazine under her mattress.

"I haven't told anyone this before," Hannah went on, picking at the edge of the duvet cover. "But my dad . . . he's not my dad."

"What?" Pippa leaned toward her.

"He told me the night before . . . the night before he left," she said. "I shouted at him and said that he couldn't just walk off, that he was my father and I needed him."

She looked around at our stunned faces.

"That's when he said it."

"What did he say, exactly?" Ella was eyeing her with suspicion.

"That he wasn't my real father," Hannah said. "Not genetically. Mum was pregnant with me when they met and they got married a couple of weeks before I was born."

"And no one had told you?"

It was clear Donna couldn't get her head around Hannah's story.

"So who *is* your dad?" Christy asked. "I mean, did your mum say?"

Ella glared at her. I could tell she was annoyed that our carefully laid plan was disintegrating before her eyes.

"I tried to ask, but she got so upset." Hannah's eyes filled with tears again. "She can't speak about any of it—not Dad . . . well, him . . . leaving, not the past—nothing."

She looked at us with wide eyes.

"And please—don't mention it to your parents because if it gets back to Mum, she might . . ."

She hesitated.

"Might what?" Donna asked.

"Go over the edge," Hannah whispered. "She feels so guilty about deceiving me all that time. That's why we moved—to have a new start."

She took a deep breath.

"The thing is, I don't feel I belong anywhere. I mean, the guy I thought was my father has disappeared off the face of the earth. . . ."

"You mean—you never get to see him?" Becky gasped. "Not ever?"

Hannah shook her head.

"Not that I want to, of course," she added hastily. "Not after what he's done. And now Mum's got a new boyfriend who's a total jerk and . . ."

"It's okay, Hannah, you've got us!" If looks could kill, Ella would have had me in a coffin in two shakes. I couldn't help it; I mean, I know I go on about my family, but at least they are there for me. And maybe we had laid into Hannah a bit too much.

"Can I see the magazine?" Hannah held out a hand toward Ella.

"Oh, I'm bored of that now!" Ella announced. "Let's tell ghost stories!"

"No, please!" Hannah crawled across the sleeping bags to where Ella was sitting. "Let me look."

What could Ella do? I could sense us all holding our breath as Hannah flicked through the pages.

"It doesn't say . . ." Her eyes scanned the "Stars" column. "I don't . . ."

"Okay, so I made it up!" Ella retorted, her face flushing. None of us looked at one another; I guess we all felt too ashamed. This hadn't been part of the plan.

"Made it up—but why?" Hannah looked genuinely bewildered.

"Why do you think?" retorted Ella. "You can't go around spreading lies about . . ."

"Hot chocolate, anyone?" I said brightly.

"Yes, please!" Christy jumped to her feet in relief. "I'll come and help."

"Me too!" Pippa rammed her feet into her

Simpsons slippers and opened the door.

"Sssh!" I whispered. "If you wake Leo, my mother is likely to go ballistic."

We crept downstairs and into the kitchen. I grabbed a packet of biscuits and ripped them open, relieved to have saved the situation. Then I heard footsteps.

"What lies?"

Hannah stood in the middle of the kitchen, looking remarkably calm and holding Ella's gaze.

"You told me that Tory thought I was a bossy cow," Ella blurted out, almost making me spill chocolate powder on the floor.

"No, I didn't." For someone facing a verbal firing squad, she was being very laid-back. "I said that Tory described you as a bossy person. Which she did."

She turned to me.

"Well? Didn't you?"

All eyes were on me.

"I said that Ella could seem bossy now and again, but I never used the word cow!"

I filled the kettle and plugged it in, trying to keep my hands from shaking. I hate rows, and this was my birthday, after all.

"Neither did I," Hannah stressed. "I don't use language like that."

"Yes, you . . ." Ella began.

"Tory's just admitted it," Hannah interrupted. "She said the words *now and again*. I said *now*, but you thought I said *cow*. . . ."

"Okay, then," interrupted Becky, seeing Ella's confused expression. "How about the fact that, according to you, Tory thinks Donna and I are slags."

"What?" Hannah looked shocked. "I said she joked about you being boy crazy—I never said . . ."

"Oh yes, you did," Becky insisted. "Didn't she, Donna?"

Donna swallowed hard and looked at the floor.

"I—well, I mean, you said she did. I didn't actually hear any of it—I was getting the drinks in, remember?"

Hannah laughed, as if she didn't have a care in the world.

"I'm not surprised you misheard," she said. "That disco was enough to shatter eardrums!"

"Chocolate's ready!" I said cheerily, praying that everyone would let the matter drop. "Who wants marshmallows on the top?"

"Dee-lish!" Hannah said, licking her lips. "Yes, please."

"Hang on!" Ella clearly wasn't going to give in without a fight. "What about the things you said about my parents?"

I have to confess, I was surprised she mentioned that—I thought she would have wanted to keep it quiet for as long as possible.

"Your parents?" Hannah blew on to her mug of chocolate. "Oh—you mean about them having problems?"

"Are they?" Christy looked up from the newspaper she had picked up. "What sort of . . ."

Ella shot her a warning look and turned back to Hannah.

"According to you, Tory said they were a total mess. . . ."

Hannah sighed.

"You've got it all wrong," she declared, so confidently that I found myself beginning to believe her. "I was just trying to be kind and understanding. What I said was that if you wanted to talk about things, I'd be there for you because I knew what it was like to have parents who messed up. That's not the same thing as saying . . ."

"Enough!" Pippa slammed her mug on to the table and stood up. "This is getting silly. Okay, so there was a misunderstanding. . . ."

"That's all it was," Hannah butted in.

"Okay." Ella nodded reluctantly. "But if you ever try to cause trouble again . . ."

"Me? Cause trouble?" Hannah appeared mortally wounded. "Okay, so maybe I interfered too much, but it was only because I wanted to be friends with you all. After my dad left, most of my old mates drifted off and . . ."

"Why would they do that?" Donna began. "It's hardly your fault if . . ."

"They just did," Hannah said, sighing slowly. "Hey, Ella, did that guy Steven really ask you out?"

I'll give her one thing—she was certainly skillful at changing the subject.

"Steven?" gasped Christy. "He asked you out? As in—out-out?"

"Is there another kind of out?" Ella teased. "Yes, but it wasn't really that he wanted to go anywhere with me. It was Alex . . ."

"Alex?" I admit it, I was miffed. I mean, don't get me wrong. I didn't fancy Alex or anything. But he had spent a lot of time with me and hardly spoken to Ella and it just showed that my deepest fears were justified. I was fourteen years and ten hours old and totally unsexy.

"Yes, Alex." Ella grinned, wiping chocolate off her mouth. "He'd persuaded Steven to . . ."

"Please! Girls!" The kitchen door flew open and my mother stood there, hair tousled and in her pajamas. "I don't want to break up the fun, but it is now half-past one in the morning! I would like to get some sleep."

"Mum!" Her timing was disastrous.

"Sorry, Mrs. Norris," Ella murmured. "We were just having a laugh. . . ."

"I know, dear, but enough is enough. Bed now or you will all be grumpy-grots in the morning!"

She can be so utterly embarrassing. It comes from being surrounded by small children all day.

We trailed back upstairs and waited until we heard the door of my parents' bedroom click shut.

"So are you going to go out with Alex?" I hissed to Ella who was on the mattress next to my bed.

"Alex?" she asked.

I held my breath waiting for her reply.

She yawned.

"Oh, I don't know—I'm too sleepy to think about

all that now," she sighed. "Let's talk about it in the morning."

"That means she hasn't made her mind up," Pippa whispered from the other side of the room.

"I'll have him if you don't want him," Becky added. "He's dead fit."

"You're going out with Warren," I reminded her, rather louder than I should have done.

"Girls! Enough!"

My father was thumping on the bedroom wall in a manner that frankly was hardly befitting of a member of the clergy.

"Not another word!"

The others seemed to fall asleep within minutes. I lay awake and wondered why my stomach was doing somersaults and why I felt like throttling Ella.

It didn't make sense.

✳ 5 ✳
Not-So-Secret Schemes

"Ella?" I whispered, leaning out of bed and shaking the heap of duvet on the floor beside me. "Are you awake?"

"I am now," she muttered grumpily. "What time is it?"

"Breakfast time," I whispered back, knowing full well that if I told her it was only seven o'clock, she would go straight back to sleep. "What about you and . . . ?"

"Why are you whispering?" she said loudly.

"Ssh," I hissed. "The others are asleep."

"Lucky them!"

"Come downstairs—we can talk better there."

Ella sighed and gazed up at me.

"It's about Alex, isn't it?" she said with a grin.

"Alex?" I tried to make it sound as if Alex was the last thing on my mind. "No, I just was wondering . . ."

"Come on!" She slipped her feet into her slippers

and began tiptoeing over the prone bodies on the floor. "You wait till you hear what I've got to tell you!"

We crept out of the room, down the stairs and into the kitchen.

"Is that the time?" Ella stared at the wall clock in disbelief. "If you'd told me it was only . . ."

"So? Get on with it."

Ella grinned.

"Steven," she said, "was put up to it by Alex. Because Alex didn't have the guts. . . ."

My heart sank. If a guy had bribed his mate to ask Ella out, he must be desperate. Not, of course, that it mattered to me either way.

". . . to ask you himself," Ella finished.

It took a moment or two for her words to hit me.

"Ask me? You mean—Alex wants me to go out with him?"

"Yup! Now can I go back to bed?"

"No, you can't!" I cried, pulling open the refrigerator door. "I'll make toasted waffles!"

"Now you're talking!" Ella perched on the edge of the kitchen table. "Do you want to hear the whole story?"

I nodded, trying not to look too eager.

"Steven said that Alex really fancied you, but he's never asked a girl out before and Steven's had loads of girlfriends. So Steven said that he was going to ask me out. . . . do you think he's fit or not? I can't make up my mind."

"Yes—no—I don't know," I replied, ripping open the waffle packet. "Go on."

"So we've decided that we will all go bowling on Tuesday!"

"What—you and me and Steven and Alex?"

Ella sighed and raised her eyebrows.

"Tory, you are so quick at times, it's frightening!" she teased. "Seven-thirty at the Superbowl."

I slammed the waffles into the toaster and slumped down on a chair opposite Ella.

"I can't."

"What do you mean, you can't?" Ella raised her eyebrows. "Oh, if it's the money, I've got some birthday cash from my aunt. . . ."

"It's not that," I told her. "I'm not allowed out on school nights for the rest of term, remember? After that little business of the biology assignment?"

"Ah." Ella looked stumped for a moment. We'd all been playing tennis down at the park most evenings for the first half of term, which was fine for the others who can scribble off assignments in ten minutes flat, but I'd got really behind and biology was the one that had to go.

It was just a pity that at the recent Parents' Evening, Mrs. Vincent took great delight in telling my father how vital biology was to my ongoing survival on the planet.

"Well," said Ella, "we'll just have to think of a way."

"Can't we just go on the weekend instead?" I said, as the waffles popped up from the toaster.

"We can't wait that long," Ella stressed. "Boys don't hang about. If we don't go, they'll get someone else to take and then. . . ."

"How come you know so much about it?" I asked her, pushing the plate of waffles toward her. "You've never been out with a boy. . . ."

"I have two older sisters, remember? I watch and learn! Anyway," Ella went on, "I know what we can do. We'll say we're going over to Pippa's to do homework."

I shook my head.

"Use your brain," I protested. "Pippa lives two minutes' walk from here and my mother is in and out of their house five times a day. We'll be caught."

"Well, Christy's then." Ella looked miffed.

"Christy has ballet on Tuesdays, so that won't work," I told her. "Let's face it, we can't go."

"That attitude is so Gemini!" Ella snarled, ladling syrup onto her waffle. "Giving up at the first hurdle! Well, I'm going anyway and . . ."

"I thought you didn't even know whether you liked Steven," I teased her.

"That's not the point," she stressed. "It's a very valuable life experience, dating boys."

She savored the last two words.

"We'll have to find someone who'll give us an alibi because then . . ."

"What about me?"

We whirled round. Hannah was standing at the door in her bathrobe.

Ella gasped. "How long have you been there?"

Hannah grinned. "Long enough. Got any more waffles?"

"You're insane!" Pippa stared at Ella and me in disbelief as we ambled down the road to church. "You are actually going to trust Hannah with something like that?"

"I think it will be okay," I ventured. "I mean,

she's so desperate to be friends with us and she overheard the whole thing, so it's safer to have her on our side. . . ."

". . . and she lives far enough away for us not to get found out. I think she wants to make up for being bitchy earlier on," Ella concluded. "She's thought it all out really well."

To be honest, I was pretty amazed at just how foolproof her plan was.

"It makes sense," Hannah had reasoned, embarking on her second waffle. "You tell your mums that you're coming to my place to help me with homework—and then if either of them phones, I'll say you've just left and call you on your mobiles to warn you!"

"And what if your mum gets to the phone first?" Ella demanded.

"She won't," Hannah replied calmly. "Because I'll be doing my homework in the study and the phone will be right by my side. No one will get to it before me!"

"Yes, but . . ."

"Listen," Hannah said calmly. "Your mum can't check with my mum beforehand anyway, because Mum's out at the wholesalers and won't be back till later. What's the problem?"

Ella and I glanced at one another and nodded.

"Agreed!" Ella announced. "And we'll phone you when we're five minutes from home, so you can relax your guard, okay?"

The scheme seemed as watertight as it could be. But now Pippa was throwing cold water on the idea.

"You should have asked one of us," she insisted as we headed toward church.

"You live too close and Christy's at ballet," I reminded her. "As for Becky and Donna . . ."

"They'd have been no good!" Christy giggled. "The moment they knew boys were involved, they'd have been there, muscling in!"

"Don't go saying that in front of Hannah," Ella warned, "or she'll tell everyone that you called them names—just the way she did with Tory."

I took a deep breath.

"Pippa, did you say I was difficult?" It had been niggling away at me ever since the previous evening, and I thought that if I asked in front of everyone, it couldn't lead to a row.

"'Course not," she said, looking hurt. "Why

would I . . . oh! Well, I did say you were jolly difficult to buy birthday presents for compared to Ella. I mean, I told her that you are book-mad but I never know what you've read. That's all."

"There!" Christy said. "That's just the way Hannah twists things. I reckon she just likes making trouble."

"And, thanks to Tory, we're lumbered with her tonight," groaned Pippa. "Sorry, Tor, I didn't mean . . ."

"It wasn't me," I pointed out. "It was my sainted mother."

It all happened when Hannah's mother turned up to collect her. Angela did the "Have you had a lovely time, poppet?" bit, and my mother did the "I don't know why they call it a sleepover because they never sleep" bit, when my father strode in to the kitchen, having finished the nine o'clock service.

"Morning, morning," he cried. He is disgustingly hearty, my father. "I'm so glad you girls are still around."

He cast his eyes round the kitchen.

"Becky and Donna not here?"

"They've gone," I told him. I didn't add that Donna had said that no way was she hanging around to get roped in to going to church with us lot.

"Not to worry," he replied breezily. "It's about FOY."

"Who is Foy?" Angela asked brightly, picking a minute piece of fluff off her fluorescent pink sundress. "Another little friend?"

In a way, it's a relief to know that other people have mothers as unreal as mine.

"It stands for Fellowship of Youth," Mum explained. "At our church—a lovely club for the teens, you know."

I could see what was coming.

"Tory, you must take Hannah along! Why didn't we think of that before?"

I heard Pippa's sharp intake of breath, and glanced at Christy. She, of course, was miles away, doodling notes of music on the back of her scrunched-up pier ticket.

"I don't think so. . . ." Hannah began.

"Oh, but you must!" My mother was never one to take no for an answer. "They do all sorts of things—cinema trips, bowling, debates, barbecues . . ."

"And the Waddle! Don't forget, the Waddle is only two weeks away!" my father declared.

"That soon? I'd forgotten. Oh, ace!" Pippa cried.

"Cool," Christy remarked, looking up for the first time. "Only, can we do the short one this time? My feet were crippled last year. . . ."

"No way!" Ella interrupted. "The whole thing— we make more money that way."

"So start getting your sponsors!" Dad finished.

Angela stood up and turned to my father.

"Douglas, dear, I don't mean to be thick, but what on earth are you talking about?"

"It's the Westbeach Waddle," my mother explained. "For charity—it's been going for hundreds of years. . . ."

"Two hundred and eighty-two, actually," my father corrected her. "It's a sort of sponsored walk these days, although of course, it all began when the local lord of the manor had to visit all his tenants in one day because . . ."

Once he gets going on history my father never stops, so I cut in.

"It's really good fun," I added. "There's the Toddle—that's just a kilometer 'round the park for little kids and buggies and things. . . ."

"I shall take Leo this year, bless him," my mother chipped in.

". . . and the Waddle, which is eight kilometers

and that's bad enough . . ." Christy interjected.

"And the Stride!" Pippa finished. "Which is twenty kilometers. . . ."

"Twenty kilometers?" Hannah's eyes bulged in her head. "I've never walked . . ."

"Everyone does it! Well, anyone with guts," Ella added, casting a pointed glance in Hannah's direction. "It's wicked—you have to go through all these checkpoints, and to make it more fun you get a list of stuff to collect."

"And that's why I need you girls at FOY tonight," my father said. "I want you to persuade as many of your friends as possible to join St. Peter's Plodders. . . ."

"Peter's what?" Ella looked aghast.

"The church team, dear," my father declared. "I've marshaled the congregation—of course, it will be a short walk for them but . . ."

"Oh, no!" I told him firmly. "If you want us to enter, we go it alone, okay? Just us and our mates. There is positively no way we're ambling along with the likes of Mrs. Meredith and . . ."

"Excellent idea!" By the way my dad grinned at my mother, I got the distinct feeling that we had been set up.

"So that will be you five and anyone else you can rustle up from FOY tonight," he murmured approvingly, scribbling some notes on a pad of paper. "You'll enjoy the club, Hannah—help you make new friends."

"I don't know," she replied. "I mean, I'm not very holy and . . ."

"Oh, that's not a problem!" my father protested. "Does this lot look holier than thou?" He waved an arm in our general direction and burst out laughing.

"That's settled then," my mother decreed, even though it wasn't.

My father nodded eagerly.

"Angela, dear, I don't suppose you'd be able to act as a marshal, would you? I've been asked to find a couple more. It's really quite a lark." He grinned conspiratorially. "We usually manage to refresh ourselves at regular intervals in a nearby hostelry!"

"When is it again?" Angela took a leather diary from her handbag.

"Saturday," my mother said. "Ten o'clock start."

"Oh—no . . . sorry, we can't do that day," Angela replied hastily. "Hannah and I are going—we have to be in London."

If I hadn't been standing right behind Hannah's mum, I wouldn't have seen the quick prod she gave Hannah.

"What a shame! Never mind, next year perhaps," Mum suggested.

"We don't *have* to go to London," Hannah pouted. "We can go there anytime."

"You know perfectly well that is the only . . . that's the day we said we'd have some mother-and-daughter time."

"You go if you want to," Hannah said firmly, shaking her head. "I'm doing the walk, okay?"

"Hannah—I'm sorry, but you are coming to London with me!"

For a moment, I thought it was going to be all-out war, but suddenly Angela had stuffed her diary back into her bag, stood up and turned to my mum.

"Kids!" she muttered, with a brittle laugh.

My mother smiled. "We wouldn't be without them, though, would we?" Judging by the expression on Angela's face, she wasn't convinced. Mind you, if I had had Hannah for a daughter, I might be of two minds.

"We'll talk about it later, Hannah," Angela

declared firmly. "Still, no harm in your going to this FAY thing. . . ."

"FOY," Hannah sighed.

"Whatever," her mother snapped. "What time should . . ."

She was interrupted by the shrilling of the front doorbell.

"Oh, heavens," Angela cried. "That'll be Toby— I left him in the car; said I'd only be a few minutes."

It was hardly surprising that Christy, Pippa, Ella, and I all suddenly decided that we simply had to go to the door to say good-bye to Hannah. Well, it would have been rude not to, wouldn't it?

"Toby, dear, I'm so sorry! Silly me—I was yabbering! Coming right away!" Angela almost fell over her own feet in her hurry to get to the door. She didn't have any luck because the rest of us were standing blocking her way, totally gobsmacked.

Toby was gorgeous. I don't mean everyday, run-of-the-mill gorgeous; I mean, breath-stopping, mind-blowing, front-cover-of-*Hunk*-type gorgeous. He was wearing frayed denim shorts and an open-neck shirt, and his suntan definitely didn't come out of a bottle.

He was, at a very conservative guess, about twenty-six years old.

"Come in, come in!" my mother was the first one to regain her composure.

"That's very nice of you." Toby smiled, revealing a perfect set of teeth. "But we have to dash. I need Angela's advice on the fittings for the hotel bathrooms. It's so important not to do twee, don't you think, especially on tiles and taps?"

My mother clearly hadn't considered the subject in much depth and my father had starting muttering about it being time for him to be getting back to the church.

"You're so right, Toby, so right!" Angela enthused, tottering down the path on her stiletto heels.

Hannah turned to me and raised her eyebrows.

"See what I mean?" she whispered.

"What do you think a guy like Toby sees in someone like Mrs. Soper?" Ella asked now, as we walked into church. "I mean, it just doesn't make sense. He's so gorgeous and she's so . . ."

"Old!" Christy said, smiling. "See you later—got to go and robe up." She waved and headed for the vestry.

"Don't forget to pray," Pippa whispered as we slid into the back pew.

"What for?" I asked.

"The success of your mad bowling scheme," she said, grinning. "It's going to need a lot of divine intervention, if you ask me."

Ella burst out laughing and got a dirty look from Mrs. Meredith, who hasn't been seen to smile since the Queen's Golden Jubilee.

"Don't mind Pippa," Ella giggled. "You're a vicar's daughter. God will be on your side."

✳ 6 ✳
Weather-beaten!

"Poor Hannah!"

I sighed and tried to look deeply anxious.

My mother looked up from her ironing.

"What's wrong with her?"

I shrugged.

"She's really struggling with our English assignment," I said, glancing at the clock and realizing that I didn't have much time to get this set up. "It must be so hard, starting at a school with a totally different syllabus from your old one."

My mother nodded sympathetically.

"Surely they're giving her extra help?" she asked, playing exquisitely into my hands.

"Not really," I replied, crossing my fingers under the table. "She was in such a state about it today that I said I'd go over and sort her out, but . . ."

"That's a great idea!" my mother said, squirting water on one of Dad's clerical shirts. "How sweet of you, Tory."

She needn't have looked quite so surprised by my kindness.

"Yes, but the assignment has to be in by tomorrow, which would mean going this evening and I'm not allowed out on school nights. . . ."

"She could come here," Mum volunteered.

I shook my head.

"Her project's on her computer and by the time she's downloaded it onto a disk and . . ."

The scale of my own inventiveness amazes me at times.

"Well, on this occasion, you can go," Mum said. "Oh, and while you're at it, take this with you to show Angela, will you?"

She handed me a table decoration made of pebbles and bits of dried seaweed with the odd flower sticking out. Just the thing I needed at the Superbowl.

I couldn't say no, and I couldn't take it. I decided to play for time.

"So you don't mind if I go?"

My mother laid down the iron and smiled at me.

"No, but you'd better get a move on. I don't want you back late—nine-thirty latest, all right?"

"Sure," I told her. It would be tight, but I reckoned we could do it.

"I'll just go and change," I said—and instantly regretted it.

"Change? What on earth for? What's wrong with those jeans?"

I thought fast.

"Not the jeans, the top," I said, heading for the door. "Smelly armpits!"

My mother burst out laughing.

"Tory, you are a funny old thing!"

I was tempted to remind her of that loving remark a few hours later.

The moment I was out of sight of my house, I speed-dialed Ella's mobile number.

"It's me—I'm on my way!"

"Me too," she hissed back. "I've phoned Hannah and read her the riot act—I reckon we're safe."

"I'll meet you at the Seagull Café in five minutes," I went on. "Couldn't put my makeup on or my mother would have guessed something was up."

By the time I had belted down Princes Avenue and on to the seafront, I was pouring with perspiration, partly from running and partly because I half expected my mother to be pursuing me with the wretched table decoration. I'd yelled a good-bye to her, slammed the door and legged it, without going into the kitchen for the usual hug and list of instructions. It seemed that I'd got away with it.

Even by the water, there wasn't a breath of air, and dark clouds loomed on the horizon. I slowed to a walk and flapped my arms in an attempt to cool down; it was going to be hard enough to look sophisticated without patches of sweat on my vest top.

"Do I look all right? Be honest!" Ella pulled me through the door of the café.

"You look great," I told her, even though I could see at once that her eyes were slightly puffy and pink. "Love the earrings."

"I made them," Ella said. "Borlotti beans, lentils, and sea glass—neat, eh?"

We bought a bar of chocolate as an excuse to use the loos, and spent the next ten minutes putting on our makeup.

"You can tell, can't you?" Ella turned to face me.

"Tell what?" I asked, because with Ella, when you're not sure of the right answer, it is best to play for time.

"Nothing," she said, dropping her lip gloss and mascara back in her bag.

I touched her arm.

"You could use a tad more concealer under your left eye," I suggested tentatively, not actually wanting to admit that it was obvious she'd been crying.

Ella nodded gratefully.

"Do you want to talk about it?" I asked.

She pulled the top off her concealer and sighed.

"It's just so awful at home," she said in a rush. "Mum cries all the time, and Dad loses his temper."

She patted concealer under her eyes with her little finger.

"And Claudia and Faith are at uni and when I try to talk to them on the phone, they just say Dad will be able to sort it, which is no help."

"Are things really bad?"

"Apparently. Dad's sold the car and we've canceled our holiday and . . ."

Ella's eyes began to fill with tears and she swallowed hard and opened her eyes wide, the way you do when you don't want the tears to squeeze out.

"Don't let's talk about it," she said emphatically. "But thanks."

She squeezed my arm.

"At least the parents are too busy with their own problems to notice where I am," she said. "Come on—let's go and work on our love lives!"

I discovered two things that evening: one) it's best not to beat boys at bowling, and two) no plan is ever watertight.

When we arrived at the Superbowl, we found Alex and Steven and Mark and Rob and two other boys we'd never met.

"This is George and that's David," Alex said. "It's okay—they're not with us."

Steven grinned, stretching out a hand to Mark. "That'll be two quid!"

The lads smirked and drifted off to a nearby lane, bowling shoes in their hands.

"Actually," Alex confided as we queued for our shoes, "they bet us that you two wouldn't turn up. I'm glad you did."

"Why? Because of the money or because of us?" Ella quipped. Not for the first time, I found myself wishing that I was as good at repartee as she was.

"I'm glad too," I told him and then realized from the look Ella gave me that I was coming on too strong.

"You're winning," Ella said to me twenty minutes later. "Miss a few!"

"No way!" I hissed back at her.

"Don't say I didn't warn you," she muttered.

I won the game.

"It's my wrist," Steven said at once. "It got hit with a cricket ball last week—it's affected my game."

"I'll start playing properly this time," Alex announced. "Didn't want to show off too much to start with."

I opened my mouth to speak, but Ella got in first.

"Let's get a drink first," she butted in quickly. "It's so hot in here. I'm sick of this heat wave."

She did look very flushed. Her fringe was sticking to her forehead and she had two spots of color on her cheeks.

"This was a crazy idea!" Alex declared, and at first I thought he was just grumpy because I'd won the game. "We choose to be in a bowling alley on the hottest night of the year—dumb or what?"

"I know," Ella said. "Why don't we give the next game a miss and go down to the beach instead?"

"Cool." Steven nodded. "You up for it Alex? Tory?"

I glanced at my watch and looked enquiringly at Ella.

"It's only eight-twenty," she said a little impatiently. "We've got heaps of time. Come on!"

We had only been on the beach for ten minutes, throwing stones in the water and playing chase the wave, when the storm broke. At first, it was just the odd flash of lightning, and even though I tried to get Ella to head for home, she told me I was being pathetic.

She changed her tune five minutes later when the heavens opened and sheets of rain began pouring down, accompanied by the kind of thunder that bursts eardrums.

I hate thunderstorms—I always have. I want to run and hide under a duvet until they've gone.

"Are you scared?" Alex took my hand as we ran up the beach, our feet slipping on the wet stones.

"Me? Of course not," I said, hoping that he wouldn't hear the wobble in my voice over the sound of the rain.

We tore across the esplanade and clambered up the steps of the bandstand to shelter. By then, Ella's hair was plastered to her face and raindrops were dripping off the end of our noses. I clamped my hands over my ears every time there was a clap of thunder and wished I was a more sophisticated person.

"Is that your phone ringing?" Alex pulled my hands away from my ears and gestured to my pocket.

Ella looked at me in alarm.

I snatched the phone, flipped open the cover, and stuck one finger in my right ear to try to drown out the sound of the rain beating on the roof of the bandstand.

"Hello?"

"It's me!" Hannah babbled. "I've been ringing for ages—why didn't you answer?"

"I just have—what's up?"

"Your mum—she phoned."

My heart began beating erratically.

"When?"

"What's happening?" Ella prodded my ribs. I waved a hand to shut her up.

"Five minutes ago," Hannah said.

"So what did you tell her?"

There was a pause.

"She's on her way to pick you up—and before

you start, I told her you had just left, like we agreed. . . ."

"And . . . ?"

"She said she'd get the car out and meet you as you walked home—because of the storm!" she told me. "She says you get really scared. . . ."

"Okay, fine. Thanks. Bye!"

I snapped the phone shut, turned to Ella, opened my mouth and closed it again. How could I get the message across to her without letting on to Alex and Steven that we were being treated like dumb kids who weren't allowed out?

"We have to go," I declared firmly. "Trouble at home. Big trouble."

Ella looked at me questioningly and I gave her a faint nod.

"I'll come with you," Alex began, as we ran down the bandstand steps and out into the rain.

"Me too," Steven added, pulling his jacket up over his head in a futile attempt to keep dry.

"No!" I didn't mean to snap, but if my mother did find us in the street with two boys when I was supposed to be studying the War Poets, there was no telling what kind of outburst there would be. "I mean, it's kind of a tricky situation and . . ."

"Well—give us your phone numbers then," Alex muttered, turning red.

"07970 546578," I gabbled. "Ella, come on!"

"Six five what?" Alex shouted after us, scribbling on the back of his hand.

"Seven eight!" I yelled.

"And mine's 07788 34 . . ."

"You can call her on mine!" I grabbed Ella's hand and we flew across the lawns to the seafront.

"We might just make it," Ella panted.

But we both knew it wouldn't be that easy.

"Wait!" Ella stopped dead at the corner of The Crescent and pulled me into a bus shelter out of the rain. "We've got to have a plan."

"We had one, remember?" I replied wryly. "It backfired."

"Not yet, it hasn't," Ella said firmly. "Now, listen— our mothers both think we are at Hannah's, right?"

"Yes." I sighed. "Come on . . ."

"Wait! But it's only your mother who is out looking for you—mine probably hasn't even noticed it's raining, the state she's in—and your mother doesn't know I was going to Hannah's as well as you, does she?"

"No, but what difference docs that make?"

"All the difference in the world," declared Ella. "So this is what we say. . . ."

We had almost made it safely to my house when my mother overtook us in her car.

"Get in!"

When my mother doesn't say "hello" or "please" or use your name, you know you're in trouble.

"And exactly *where* have you been? I've been 'round the block a dozen times."

"At Hannah's," we chorused in unison.

"Oh, really?" My mother looked from me to Ella and back again. "And when did you leave Hannah's house?"

"Ages ago," Ella said swiftly. "We knew we had to be home in good time—only then the rain came. . . ."

". . . and neither of us had a coat, so we stood in the bus shelter . . ."

". . . and Tory got really scared—she was hyperventilating and everything. . . ."

This was the part of the story I didn't approve of. It made me sound such a wimp; I've never hyperventilated in my life. Mind you, when I caught the expression on my mother's face, I thought that perhaps there was a first time for everything.

". . . so we waited until . . ."

"Will you stop these lies *this minute*?" My mother rammed the car into gear and did a three-point turn. Well, seven-point actually; driving is not one of her best skills.

"I'll drop you home, Ella," she said abruptly. "Before your poor mother has anything else to worry about."

"Thank you," Ella murmured meekly.

My mother thundered on.

"I phoned Hannah and she said you had both left—not that I knew, of course, that Ella was meant to be there. If I had . . ."

I sent a quick arrow prayer to God to stop my mother from saying something derogatory.

For once, he answered.

"Anyway," my mother said, "I decided to come and meet you both because it was so wet and I knew that Tory . . ."

"You must have missed us when we were in the bus shelter," I interrupted rapidly before she had the chance to list my phobias again.

"It's a good story, Victoria," my mother said. "But it won't wash, because the lightning set the burglar alarm off."

"Pardon?"

"At the hotel—it was clanging away like crazy. I was just getting into the car, thinking I should phone back to tell Angela, when she and Toby pulled up outside."

"Oh."

"Oh, indeed!"

"How did they know it was ringing?" Ella asked. "You can't possibly hear it from Sackville Road."

She gets more like Pippa every day.

"It's linked to Toby's mobile," Mum said. "Isn't modern technology wonderful?"

"How does that work then?" I gabbled, thinking that she was starting to soften up.

She slowed down and pulled into a parking space outside Ella's house.

"I don't know and it's hardly relevant right now, is it?"

Mum rammed on the hand brake, and turned to face me.

"I told Angela that I was just off to meet you two and . . ."

She didn't need to finish. We'd blown it.

"When Hannah's mother said you hadn't been there all evening, how do you think I felt?"

"Sorry . . ."

"Oh, sorry, is it? You will be, young lady. I should have realized something was up when you went off without taking the flower arrangement, or coming for a hug or anything."

She leaned across and opened the passenger door.

"Ella, I don't know whether your mother knows what's been going on and it's none of my business. Her rules are her rules."

She made it sound as if Mrs. Foster was the personification of decadent parenthood.

"But I suggest you get in the house now and put her mind at rest."

"Yes, Mrs. Norris." Ella mouthed the words "ring me" through the window and ran up the path to her house.

"So, Victoria? Exactly where have you been?"

I had no choice but to tell her the truth. And, the moment I began, I saw my freedom, my future, and my social life evaporate in a flash.

✳ 7 ✳
Truth Time

"**What happened?** You didn't ring me!"

Ella cornered me at the school gate the following morning.

"My mobile doesn't have a signal in the house, and my mother banished me to my room after she'd lectured me for half an hour."

"So—what happened?" Ella repeated.

I sighed. "Grounded. I'm not allowed out until the Waddle."

"Did you tell her the whole truth?"

"Not the beach bit," I admitted as the registration bell rang. "I just said we'd been bowling with a couple of guys who used to go to drama club. I thought that the drama club thing might make her a bit less mad."

"Did it?"

"No."

Ella sighed.

"I feel really guilty," she murmured as we filed into the main building.

"Why? We both agreed to do it—it's not your fault."

"I don't mean that," she said. "It's just that your mum has grounded you and my mum didn't turn a hair. She just said that it proved her point about raincoats—or something equally bizarre."

"Lucky you!" I felt a stab of envy until I remembered that Ella's mother was probably beside herself with worry about something more important than an evening's bowling.

"Anyway, where's Hannah?" I glanced round the crowded locker room. "You have to admit—she did her best."

Ella nodded.

"I hope she didn't get into trouble on our account," she added. "With her mum, I mean."

"We must find her and check," I agreed. "At least we know she's on our side at last."

Famous last words.

Hannah didn't come to school that day. We didn't give it much thought, because Christy was off and so was Donna; they both had the tummy bug that had been doing the rounds of Year Eight, and we guessed Hannah must have got the same thing.

At three-fifteen that afternoon, we learned the truth.

Mrs. Temple called us to her desk as she finished our PHSE lesson.

"I've had Hannah's mother on the phone," she began.

"Is Hannah okay?" I asked hastily, pushing aside the niggling feeling that Mrs. Temple didn't usually feel the need to discuss our classmates' health with us.

"From what I understand from Mrs. Soper, Hannah is very distressed." Mrs. Temple peered at us over the top of her rimless spectacles. "So distressed, in fact, that she couldn't face school today."

She coughed and tapped her pen on the table.

"I never had you two down as bullies."

"Bullies? Us?" Ella at least managed to articulate her thoughts. I, on the other hand, was speechless.

"Apparently, you forced Hannah to tell lies in order to cover up your own deceptions," Mrs. Temple stated, eyeing us closely. "I am very disappointed in you both."

"That's not fair!" Ella burst out. "It was Hannah's idea. . . ."

"Ella, I am not interested in the petty details of

your little schemes," Mrs. Temple said, making a pyramid out of her fingers and tapping her nose thoughtfully. "What concerns me is that Hannah felt she had to do what you said because otherwise, you said you would refuse to be her friends and make her life hell."

"That is so not true!" I butted in. "Honestly, Mrs. Temple . . ."

"I chose you, Victoria, to look after Hannah because I'd always thought you were a sympathetic, friendly sort of girl. I'm sure your father would be horrified. . . ."

It was always the same. Because I'm a vicar's daughter, I'm supposed to be such a goody-goody. Life was a lot easier when Dad was an IT manager.

"Mrs. Temple, may I say something? Please?" Ella pulled herself to her full height and held the tutor's eye. "It really is important."

Mrs. Temple gestured to us to follow her down the corridor and into one of the study bays.

"Well?" She sat down heavily on one of the chairs and we followed suit. "I'm listening."

Ella told her the truth. Just as it happened. Every detail.

". . . so you see, Mrs. Temple, I know we were

wrong, and Tory's mum's grounded her . . ."

"I'm not surprised," Mrs. Temple cut in dryly.

". . . but we didn't ask Hannah to cover for us. She was eavesdropping on us when we were in Tory's kitchen, and she offered."

Mrs. Temple didn't say anything, but then again, she didn't argue with us.

"Even then, we weren't sure we could trust her," I added.

"And we've been proved right," Ella muttered under her breath.

Mrs. Temple stood up.

"I think you had better leave this with me," she said. "It seems there is fault on both sides. But you know that life has been difficult for Hannah and . . ."

Maybe she caught the glance that passed between Ella and me, or maybe she remembered that she had been sworn to secrecy.

"Did you or did you not threaten to break friends with Hannah unless she did what you said?"

I shook my head.

"No way," I stressed. "I swear it. . . ."

"On the Bible," Ella added.

Mrs. Temple sighed.

"Run along then," she told us. "I've no doubt your mothers will have something to say about this. And remember—from now on . . ."

I knew what was coming.

"Be nice to Hannah," she finished.

"You can't say I didn't warn you," Pippa said as she, Ella, and I walked home. "That girl is a liability."

"What I don't get," Ella said, "is why she would go telling tales to Mummy if she's supposed to want to be our mate?"

"Maybe her mother got shirty with her and she wanted to push the blame on to us," I suggested. "Ben and Danny do it all the time."

"Ben and Danny," interrupted Ella, "are little kids. Hannah's fourteen."

"I never could understand what you saw in her in the first place," remarked Becky, who in the absence of Donna had deigned to walk home with us. "She's so drippy."

"Whatever," Pippa said impatiently. "She's had it as far as I'm concerned."

"Good decision." Becky nodded. "So, go on—tell us about last night."

Ella gave her a withering look.

"You know about last night," she said. "We got into trouble. . . ."

"Not that!" Becky urged. "The guys—how did it go? Did they ask you out again?"

"No." Ella sighed. "But they have got Tory's phone number. Have you checked your mobile, Tory?"

I'd been checking it every fifteen minutes throughout the day.

"Nothing," I said.

"Bad sign," murmured Becky.

"Not that it matters," I said, ignoring her. "I'm grounded anyway."

"I'm not," stressed Ella. "Anyway, you're mum's bound to soften after a couple of days."

"You clearly don't know my mother," I replied.

"Don't worry, Angela dear. I'll speak to Tory as soon as . . . ah, here she is now!"

The look my mother gave me as she put the phone down was the kind you see on TV just before the murderer stabs his victim.

"What's all this about you bullying . . . ?" she began.

I sighed and repeated the whole story, just like

we had to Mrs. Temple. It took forever, but my mother didn't yell anymore.

"I can't imagine Hannah's mother would make a fuss unless there was a good reason," she said thoughtfully.

"Hannah did say that her mum was on the edge," I told her. "Perhaps she's just overreacting."

"Maybe," my mother murmured. "She always was a bit of a drama queen. . . ."

She checked her words.

"All right, leave it with me. But from now on . . ."

"We'll be nice to Hannah."

Between Mum and Mrs. Temple, I guessed things would get sorted. After all, that's what mothers and teachers are for.

Hannah didn't come back to school until Friday. I had been relieved when she was still away on the Thursday because, as Ella pointed out, we were in a pretty tricky position.

"If we refuse to speak to her, we'll have Mrs. T and her mother on our case again," she reasoned over lunch in the cafeteria. "And if we're all mega-friendly, she'll think she's got away with it."

Pippa was, as usual, the one with the bright idea.

"Christy will sort it," she declared, stuffing chips down her throat as if they were going out of fashion.

"I will?" Christy, still pale from her gastric bug, toyed halfheartedly with her cheese roll. "How?"

"You weren't here when it all blew up in our faces," Pippa said. "So you can be all friendly and chat to Hannah—ask questions, find out just what she did and didn't say."

"But what will I say?" Christy asked vaguely.

"Use your imagination," Pippa ordered her sternly. "Be creative."

As it happened, she didn't have to. On Friday morning, just before attendance, Ella, Pippa, Becky, and me were all jostling for the mirror in the locker room when Hannah appeared. She looked pale and had dark lines under her eyes.

"Before you say a single word," she began, dashing up to Ella and me, "I am so, so sorry."

"For what?" Ella didn't even turn to face her, but merely went on piling on the lip gloss.

"My mother's behavior," Hannah thundered. "I really tore her off a strip—how dare she go blabbing to Mrs. Temple like that!"

I shot a glance toward Pippa, who had been edging closer in order to catch what Hannah was saying.

"Well, she couldn't have blabbed, as you put it, if you hadn't dropped us in it in the first place, could she?" Ella argued, moving to one side so that I could see in the mirror.

"I didn't," Hannah retorted. "It was that wretched burglar alarm—my mother saw your mum when . . ."

"We know all that," I interrupted, raising my voice over the shrilling of the first registration bell. "That didn't mean you had to say that we'd forced you into lying for us, did it? It was your idea in the first place."

"I probably didn't handle it very well," Hannah admitted. "It's just that Mum went ballistic when she found out."

I found that hard to believe; I wouldn't have thought "Poppet" could do any wrong.

"I mean—way over the top," Hannah went on. "Yelling and saying that she had enough to cope with without me turning into a liar like my father."

She paused and saw she had our attention.

"So of course, I blew a gasket and said it was

hardly likely that I was going to turn out like him, since he wasn't my real father in the first place, and then she burst into tears and just wouldn't stop crying and I felt like a real cow."

"What," asked Becky, rubbing concealer onto a zit, "has all this got to do with you turning on Ella and Tory?"

"Mum asked me why I'd been so stupid as to agree to cover up for them, and I told her . . ."

"Yes?"

"I said that I knew that, if I did nice things for you lot, then I would be one of the crowd and you'd be my mates. She's always going on about wanting me to make friends and I thought that would get me off the hook."

"Me, me, me . . ." muttered Ella under her breath.

"But that's all I said. Honestly." Hannah looked at us pleadingly.

None of us said a word. For my part, I wanted to believe her; I knew how parents could react in totally irrational ways to the smallest things. And there was still that niggling feeling that there was more to Hannah's life than any of us knew about; Mrs. Temple's words still resonated in my head.

"You do believe me, don't you?" Hannah pleaded.

"I guess," I said tentatively.

"No," declared Becky.

"Yes—no—oh, I don't know what to believe with you," Ella muttered.

At that moment, the second registration bell rang and as one, we turned and clattered up the stairs.

"So can we be friends?" Hannah was panting along behind us.

"Sssh!" Becky ordered her. "No talking after second bell."

Even Hannah was speechless. It must have been the first time in living memory that Becky had kept a school rule.

"I've brought the photos!" Hannah said at lunchtime as we queued for the cafeteria. "There are some ace ones of you!"

"What photos?" I wasn't sure whether I was prepared to be chatty with her or not.

"From the pier party, silly," she said, pulling some pictures from the envelope. "Look at this one—you and Ella eating candyfloss."

"What about me and candyfloss?" Ella came up behind us. "Hey—let's see. These are stunning!"

They were very good photos. There was Pippa wagging her finger at me, which is something she does a great deal, and Ella dancing like someone possessed, and a great one of Christy staring into space, which is something she does a lot too.

"Can I borrow the negatives?" I asked casually as I flicked through them.

"You mean, can you borrow the negatives with Alex in them, don't you?" Ella teased. "Going to get them blown up to poster size, are you?"

I dug her in the ribs. Sometimes, it's as if Ella can read your thoughts.

"Sure—take the lot!" Hannah said airily. "Pass them around and give them back when you've finished. There's a one-hour photo place next to the newsagents on Sackville Road."

It was as we were going back to class at the end of the lunch hour that Ella looked over her shoulder and then leaned toward me.

"If I give you the money, will you get me an eight by twelve of that one of me and . . ."

"You and Pippa? You and Christy?" I teased. "Or could it possibly be you and Steven?"

"It's only because it's a good picture of me!" she retorted. "And besides, it's a souvenir."

"Of what?"

"The first time a guy kissed me," she said, grinning.

"Ella! He didn't . . ."

"He did. Well, a peck anyway. It's a start."

I was shocked. Well, all right, not shocked. Jealous. Not that I wanted Alex to kiss me or anything. Not yet.

But he might have tried.

"I think we should give her another chance," I began during afternoon break. We'd decided to go into a huddle in the sports hall and sort out what to do about Hannah once and for all.

"You always say that," said Pippa. "You're too soft."

"But think about all this business with her father," I urged her. "It must have scrambled her brain . . ."

"What brain would that be?" Ella asked innocently.

"Imagine not even knowing where your father is," I finished. "How unreal is that?"

"Unreal is about right," Pippa stressed. "The whole thing seems a bit odd to me."

"Why? Loads of parents split up," Christy commented.

"Not that bit," Pippa said. "The bit about him not being her dad in the first place. I mean, think about it; if he wasn't, surely she would have known years ago. What about birth certificates and stuff?"

"I don't know about all that," I admitted, a bit miffed that I hadn't thought of that. "She says she doesn't want to see him, but my guess is that she's missing him something rotten. You'd think he'd write or something. And when I confronted her, she did say that she had tried to stick up for us. . . ."

"Well, she would say that, wouldn't she?" Pippa interjected.

"Tory has a point," Christy said, doing *pliés* against the wall bars. "I mean, it sounds to me as if her mother just overreacted—mine does it all the time."

"Besides, we're lumbered with her for the Westbeach Waddle," I went on. "No way am I going to face the Spanish Inquisition from my parents if I try to ditch her next Saturday."

Ella sighed.

"True," she said. "It wouldn't be fair for Tory to get into trouble because we've blanked Hannah."

"Can you imagine," groaned Pippa, "walking twenty kilometers with Hannah whining all the time?"

"Maybe she'll go off with some of the others from FOY," I began.

"Hang on," Ella teased. "That's where this all started, remember? You saying Hannah would meet someone at the pier party. . . ."

"And the only people who met anyone new were you two!" laughed Christy. "By the way, how is the love life?"

I sighed. "It's not. They never rang back."

"Perhaps they lost the number," Pippa reasoned. "You know what guys are like for . . ."

"The number!" Ella cried. "The rain—his hand—that's it! That's why!"

Pippa gazed at her.

"Perhaps you could repeat that using conventional English?" she demanded.

"Tory was in such a panic to get home . . ." she began.

"Blame me, why don't you?" I muttered.

". . . and she shouted out the phone number and Alex wrote it on the back of his hand. He's clearly lost it!"

"His hand?" asked Christy, who had moved on to a few *battements*.

"Ha, ha! Very witty! No, the number—it will have been washed off in all that rain. He's probably desperate to reach you—and, of course, Steven won't be able to contact me. . . ."

She looked at me in desperation.

"What shall we do?"

"We can't *do* anything," I told her. "We can't just ring up and say 'Hey, we know you want to see us, really, so here we are!'"

"We can't ring up and say anything," sighed Ella. "I lost their numbers."

"I've got Alex's," I said, somewhat smugly, I admit.

Three pairs of eyes turned and looked at me in utter disbelief.

"You have got Alex's number?" Ella repeatd slowly. "He gave you his number?"

I shook my head.

"No—but it will be in my drama club yearbook," I said. "It's just struck me. Not that he's in my group anymore, but I guess his number won't have changed from last year."

"Now she tells us!" Ella grinned at me. "So phone him."

"I can't—what do I say?"

"Do you think she'll want to do the whole twenty kilometers?"

Christy shook her wrists and ankles and sat cross-legged on the floor.

We looked at her in amazement.

"Hannah, I mean," she added, realizing that the conversation had moved on.

"That's it! Christy, you're a star!" Ella cried. "Do it, Tory!"

"Do what?" There are times when I find Ella's train of thought very hard to follow.

"Ring Alex, invite the guys to come on the Waddle," she said. "I'll even shut up about Hannah if you get Steve—well, all the lads—to come along."

"Do we really want boys along?" argued Pippa.

Christy grinned. "Is the Pope a Catholic?"

Ella pulled a face.

"Ring Alex the minute you get in, Tory," she urged.

"What shall I say?" I couldn't help thinking it all sounded a bit contrived to me.

"You'll think of something," Ella said confidently as we traipsed back across the yard to the main building. "Just do it."

❋ 8 ❋
Up—and Down

It took me ages to pluck up the courage to phone Alex and, when I did, he was out.

"Any message?" the woman on the other end, who I assumed was his mother, asked politely.

"Can you just say that Tory phoned? It's about drama club."

I hoped his mother wouldn't ask too many questions.

"My number is 07970 546578," I told her. "Thanks!"

All evening I jumped every time my phone rang, but each time it was Ella asking the same question.

"Have you spoken to him yet?"

"No!" I snapped after her fifth phone call. "And if you don't get off the line, he won't be able to get through."

"I've being trying creative visualization for the past hour," Ella told me. "It's in my new magazine. You have to close your eyes and imagine a TV screen in front of you and then you play out the scene you want to happen. And it does!"

"Oh, sure!" There were times when Ella's airy-fairy ideas got to me.

"Go on, we'll both try it. Do it now. Picture Alex asking you out. . . ."

"Tory!" Mum's voice wafted up from below.

"Sorry, got to go—Mum's calling," I told Ella. "You visualize away there and maybe it will be you he phones!"

I thundered down the stairs, tripping over a couple of Space Invaders and a toy fire engine and saying what my father would call a totally unnecessary word as I did so.

Standing in the hall, with my mother eyeing him warily, was Alex.

"It worked!" I gasped under my breath. Ben and Danny were peering 'round the kitchen door, surveying the scene with interest.

"Hi," Alex said, shifting from one foot to the other. "Are you okay?"

"Fine," I nodded. Sadly, the word came out as a high-pitched squeak.

"And you are?" My mother was about to start one of her famous interrogations.

"Alex—Alex Bartholomew," he replied. "It was me Tory went bowling with on Tuesday."

"Oh, was it now?" My mother eyed him up and down. "Still, you weren't to know, I suppose."

"Pardon?" Poor Alex looked thoroughly bewildered.

"Would you like a drink?" I cut in fast before my mother could do any more damage.

"Good idea!" My mother had no choice but to agree; she's always telling me that good manners cost nothing. That, and being kind to the entire universe. "Tea? Chocolate? Cola?"

"Chocolate, please," Alex replied.

As Mum bustled ahead of us into the kitchen, Alex slipped something into my hand.

"I brought this back. I think you dropped it the other evening."

It was a diamanté hair clip.

"Thanks—but I don't think . . ." I faltered and decided not to admit right now that I thought it must be Ella's—Alex might just take it into his head to march off 'round to her house.

"I want chocolate!" Ben began.

"Not now, darling," my mother told him. "It's bedtime."

Ben opened his mouth to yell but Alex got in first.

"I say—is that a tyrannosaurus rex?" he asked, squatting down and examining Ben's plastic dinosaur.

"No, silly, it's a brontosaurus, don't you know anything?" Danny interrupted.

Alex sighed. "Not much, but you obviously do."

My mother gazed at him admiringly as she made the drinks. Anyone who is nice to the boys is an automatic winner with her, and for once I was glad the little monsters were around.

"Are you Tory's boyfriend?" Danny asked.

The gladness evaporated in an instant.

"Danny, shut it!" I could feel myself blushing. "Mum, can't you . . ."

For once in her life, my mother was ahead of me.

"Upstairs, you two! Tory, make the chocolate—I'll be back in two ticks."

Since I was quite sure that she meant every word of it, I thought it best to get straight to the point. Alex clearly thought the same.

"I'm sorry I didn't . . ." he began.

"I tried to phone you . . ." I started at precisely the same moment.

"Sorry, after you," he said, smiling.

"No, it's okay—you go ahead."

Alex dropped his eyes and began to take a close interest in the floor tiles.

"I wanted to phone you but I lost your number—well, I think I wrote it down wrong and anyway by the time I got home it was all smudged."

"So how did you find out where I live?" I asked, stirring the chocolate.

"Your friend told me," he said. "Can't remember her name—she was at the pier party."

"Ella? Pippa?" I began, but Alex shook his head.

"No, the dark-haired one . . ."

I gasped. "Hannah?"

"That's it!" he nodded. "She lives in the same block of flats as my gran. I didn't know that, of course, until I bumped into her in the lift earlier, otherwise I'd have come 'round sooner."

Alex sipped his chocolate and put the mug on the table.

"She said she hadn't got your phone number but told me where you lived," he said.

I knew she had got my phone number but I didn't care. Face-to-face beat the telephone any day.

"Actually," I ventured, "the hair clip isn't mine." I don't wear hair jewelry; it's not my style.

"I know," Alex admitted, turning to look out of the window. "I needed an excuse to come over."

"You mean . . . ?"

"I bought it," he gabbled. "Late birthday pressie. But it's okay, I know it's naff and I mean, you can ditch it and . . ."

"It's gorgeous," I breathed. And suddenly, it was.

I decided that I was, actually, very much into hair jewelry.

After Alex left, I had the distinct feeling that I was walking on air, and that no matter what the universe decided to hurl at me, nothing would stop me feeling like a million dollars. I even went upstairs and hugged my brothers and read them three whole pages of the latest Harry Potter, because I was so grateful to Ben for falling over and hitting his head on the bath, which had prevented my mother from coming downstairs for a whole twenty minutes while she pacified him.

A lot happened in that twenty minutes. Alex said he'd like to see me again, and I had to confess that I was grounded until the Waddle and then he said that he'd never taken part in the Waddle before and I said, Why don't you?

And he said he'd like that if I was waddling too.

And then we got the giggles.

I told him that a whole group of us were going on the walk, and that's when I remembered Ella.

"I don't suppose Steven would like to come along too, would he?" I asked, ferreting around in the freezer for the remains of the banoffi ice cream I knew was there.

"Why?" Alex asked abruptly. "Do you like him?"

"Ella fancies him," I replied, shoving the tub of ice cream on the table and offering Alex a spoon.

"She does? He's got this thing that girls never like him. He goes out with someone a couple of times and then they dump him."

I laughed.

"Well, I can assure you this one won't! And it's her birthday on Saturday, so we might do something after as well. Do you think he'll come?"

Alex nodded.

"Sure." He grinned. "Try keeping him away. In fact, I'll get a crowd of us together. Are we going to do the full twenty kilometers?"

"Of course!" I replied. "It'll be a real laugh!"

"So you see," I told Ella on the phone later that evening, "that settles it. If it hadn't been for Hannah, Alex wouldn't have found me and you wouldn't be getting to walk twenty kilometers with the amazing Steve!"

"You're right," she agreed. "Though why she didn't just give him your phone number and have done with it . . ."

"Oh, come on, stop looking for trouble!" I retaliated, because frankly I was getting bored with the whole Hannah thing. "It's nearly the end of term, we'll hardly see the girl in the holidays and anyway, next Friday she'll probably . . ."

". . . find someone else!" Ella burst out laughing. "Okay, you win. Do you think he's a Taurus?"

"Who?"

"Steve, of course!"

"How should I know?" I asked. "Does it matter?"

"Of course it matters!" Ella exploded. "What if we're not compatible? I think we are, though, don't you? I mean, unless he's an Aries or . . ."

I let her babble on while I held the phone to my left ear and gazed at my reflection in my dressing-table mirror, wondering why I looked exactly the same as I had two days ago.

I thought falling in love was meant to make your skin glow and your hair shine.

I was clearly an exception to the rule.

I didn't see anything of the others that weekend, because Pippa was in Hampshire visiting her gran, Christy had a music festival in Worthing, and Ella had gone to see one of her sisters at university. Not that it would have made much difference if they'd all been there since I was totally grounded.

I say totally. When we ran out of milk on Saturday morning, my mother was perfectly happy to send me to the shop for some more; when Dad left his draft sermon in the church hall, it was me who had to stop watching MTV and go and retrieve it and, of course, me who got roped into taking the boys to the park while my parents went to some lunchtime drinks party.

I thought I might have earned some Brownie points for being so helpful, but I should have known better. Later that afternoon, I was in my bedroom, supposedly doing Biology but, in fact, gazing at the photo of me and Alex in the dodgem car that I'd collected on the way home from school the day before. I was just debating whether to frame it or simply to keep it under my pillow, when my mother walked in. She never knocks—and even if she had, it probably wouldn't have made any difference.

"Clean towels, darling," she said, dumping them on the end of my bed. "What have you got there?"

You know how your fate can be sealed in a nano-second? Because I haven't inherited my mother's devious mind, I just handed her the picture.

"It's me and Alex at the dodge . . ."

That's when my brain clicked in.

"It's very good of you," she said, but she wasn't smiling. "So, once again, you went against my express wishes, did you?"

I gulped.

"Mum, it was fine—there were floodlights and it was perfectly safe and . . ."

"Tory, you know full well that only ten days ago a couple of girls were mugged for their bags down by the funfair," she said. "One of them is still in the hospital. I don't try to be difficult . . ."

You could have fooled me.

". . . but one can't be too careful. I gave in about the party—against my better judgment, I might add—but I said you had to stay on the pier."

"Sorry," I mumbled.

"Pity," she said. "I was going to tell you that I'd had second thoughts about grounding you during this glorious weather. But, since I can't trust you to leave the house without breaking a rule, it's best that you stay in."

"Mum, that is so not fair! Didn't you ever do something just for the hell of it?"

She looked at me in astonishment. Stupid question.

"Remember what Gran used to say?" I was really pushing my luck here, but reckoned I had nothing to lose.

"What?" My mother frowned.

"She said that you were a real tearaway when you were sixteen," I reminded her. "Something about a motorbike and the boy from the corner shop—and wasn't there a story about you trying to climb in through the kitchen window one evening so she wouldn't know you'd skived off—only you got stuck and had to call for help. I've never done that."

To my surprise, Mum was smiling. And then, suddenly, she burst out laughing.

"Tory, Tory, Tory!" she said. "What am I going to do with you?"

"Let me off the hook?" I pleaded.

She gave me a hug.

"I sometimes forget you're growing up," she said with a sigh. "And I sometimes forget what it's like to be a teenager."

She paused.

"It seems so long ago that I was . . . oh well! Okay—I relent. Grounding over! I think you've learned your lesson."

I gave her a hug and made a mental note to apologize to God for telling him that he was never on my side.

* 9 *
Bugs and Bombshells

In the event, it wouldn't have made much difference whether I had been grounded or not, because the following Tuesday I got the tummy bug, and spent two days quietly dying. Even on Thursday, when I had stopped throwing up and dashing to the loo, I decided two periods of Biology and a cross-country run would almost certainly bring on a relapse and so I refused all food, knowing that was a sure way to get another day off.

I was in my bedroom that afternoon, supposedly catching up on missed homework, but actually sending text messages to everyone I'd ever met, when the doorbell rang. I didn't take any notice— we get loads of parishioners coming to see my father and I'm supposed to stay out of the way in case they are having a trauma and bursting into tears all over the place.

But then I heard Ella's mother in the hall below, so I turned my stereo down low enough for me to eavesdrop, but not so low that my mother would notice, and edged out onto the landing.

"Debbie, can you spare a minute? I need to talk." Even I could tell from Mrs. Foster's voice that this was serious.

"Of course, dear—come through to the kitchen."

If it hadn't been for what Ella's mum said next, I would have given up and gone back to my room.

"It's Ella I'm really worried about. . . ."

I thought I must have missed something crucial by being off school—the others hadn't come near me because, believe me, they didn't want what I had. Even Christy, who had already had it, settled for sending me notes and peppermints to take away the taste of the sick. I'd had loads of text messages, though, and no one had said a thing about any problems; all Ella's messages had been about whether to have a barbecue or a swim party after the walk.

"I've hardly slept a wink," I heard Ella's mum say. As the kitchen door closed behind them, I sped down the stairs, kicking off my shoes so that I wouldn't make any noise. Thankfully, the boys were with friends down the road and Leo was asleep. For once.

". . . the other two, you see, are at university—it won't affect them so much. . . ."

I tiptoed closer to the kitchen door, pushing open the loo door on the way in case I needed a quick escape.

"Selling the house is bad enough," I heard Ella's mum say, and then her voice cracked. "But if we have to leave Westbeach . . ."

"No!" I had to clamp my hand over my mouth to stop the word escaping.

"Leave? Are you sure?"

There was a lot more low muttering that I couldn't hear before my mother chipped in.

"And Ella? Has she taken it really badly?"

I held my breath.

"We haven't told her yet," Mrs. Foster admitted. "She knows things are bad financially, that's nothing new. That's why we had to stop educating her privately."

My mother said nothing. I knew her views on private schools.

"She knows we may have to sell the house, but when I tell her that she may have to leave all her friends . . ."

"But why?" my mother broke in. "I mean, there

are some really nice small houses in Westbeach, very reasonable, or perhaps one of those flats down by the park."

"Debbie, it's not that simple. We're not just hard up. Andrew may have to declare himself bankrupt."

"Oh!" I could tell even through a closed door that my mother was lost for words. Which made two of us.

There was a lot more talk about money and stocks and shares and failed business ideas, and I was about to go back upstairs and think everything through when I heard my name.

"I just want to make sure Tory will be around when we tell her. Ella relies on Tory so much."

This was news to me. Of all my mates, Ella was the one who seemed totally self-sufficient, the one with an answer for everything and a solution for every problem. For a moment, I felt a warm glow.

"In fact, Ella confessed that Tory's the only person she's mentioned any of this to," Ella's mum said. "Has Tory spoken to you?"

"No," Mum replied.

"Well, that just goes to show how discreet she is," said Ella's mum. "Oh, it's all such a horrid mess!"

I heard the sound of tissues rustling and felt like crying myself. They couldn't move; life without Ella just wouldn't be the same.

"The thing is, Andrew's brother up in Newcastle has offered him a job," said Ella's mum. "We don't want to go, but we need the money. And if we're going to go, we've got to do it soon. Before the start of the new school year."

That's when it really hit me. By September, Ella might not be here.

"You're going to have to tell her soon, Ginny," my mother said firmly. "There are only two weeks of term left—she has a right to know."

"Don't you think I realize that?" Ella's mum sobbed. "It's just that I keep hoping something will turn up—we'll win the Lottery or . . ."

"Now, that really is being silly!" my mother replied. "Waste of money, lottery tickets, believe me."

I heard her sigh.

"Are you sure Andrew couldn't get a job in Westbeach?"

"He probably could," Ella's mum said. "But it's all down to pride—he says he couldn't stand seeing all his old colleagues and friends every day, knowing they knew he'd messed up."

"If his friends are true friends, then it won't matter," Mum said. "Mind you, men are more like that than us women—and I can't imagine that Ella and Tory will fall out just because she has to move."

There are times when I realize that my mum is something special. But, even as I thought that, my eyes filled with tears. Newcastle was the other end of the country—you could hardly pop round for a pizza and a makeup session after school.

I heard chairs scraping against the tiled floor and guessed that Mrs. Foster was about to leave. I sped down the hall and into the loo, being careful not to shut the door completely.

"I guess we'll tell Ella on Sunday—after this walk and everything," I heard Mrs. Foster say. "She's so excited about it—between you and me, I think there might be a lad involved."

"I should think," murmured my mother, "that is highly likely. Tory's just discovered boys."

Honestly, she made it sound like I'd been totally gender-unaware all my life.

"Don't worry," Mum went on. "I am sure something will turn up and I won't say a word to Tory about the house move, not until you say so. I'm so sorry, Ginny dear. You must let us know if there's anything . . ."

Fortunately, my mother had opened the door and walked to the gate with Ginny, so I was able to run upstairs and to my room without being seen. My heart was thumping and I felt slightly sick, partly at the thought of losing Ella, but also because I was going to have to act like nothing was wrong—and I wasn't sure I could do that.

"Tory!" My mum was calling me as the front door slammed behind her. Surely she wasn't going to break the confidence and tell me everything now?

I went downstairs, trying to look perfectly normal.

"You still look a little pale, darling," she began.

"I'm fine," I assured her, wanting to get away so that I could think things through.

"Fresh air, that's what you need," Mum declared. "Why not go and see Ella after tea? Catch up on all the news you've missed."

"I'll see her at school in the morning," I said hastily. "I've got loads of work to finish off."

My mother looked amazed.

"I thought you'd like to get out. Make the most of . . . this lovely weather."

Make the most of the time you have with her. That's what Mum really meant to say.

And I wanted to. It was just that I didn't know how I was going be with Ella and not burst into tears and tell her everything.

It was safer to stay at home.

✳ 10 ✳
Making Waves

"Personally, I think Hannah's mother is quite wrong," I heard my mother say on Friday morning, as I packed my schoolbag with one hand and ate an apple with the other. "You can't make a fourteen-year-old do things she doesn't want to."

It never stopped you trying, I thought wryly, shoving the last folder into my bag and struggling with the zip.

"Besides, I think Hannah would enjoy the Waddle—she seems a shy little thing . . ."

Which shows how much you know, I thought. I was feeling out of sorts and picky; I had dreamed that I was waving good-bye to Ella and she suddenly disappeared in a puff of smoke and I was the only one who noticed.

". . . and surely Hannah can see her father any time?" Mum concluded. "What's so special about tomorrow?"

I choked on a piece of apple that had gone down

the wrong way. This I had to investigate.

". . . really none of our business, dear," my father was saying as I ambled into the kitchen.

"Did you say Hannah's not coming tomorrow?" I asked innocently. "Why not?"

"She's going to see her father," my mother said, wiping Ready Brek off Leo's chin.

"I thought I heard her say she never saw her dad," I ventured, not wanting to be too specific and stop the conversation dead in its tracks.

"Then it's all the more pleasing that they're building bridges, isn't it?" my father said, in a tone of voice that suggested the discussion was over. "Come on, boys—clean your teeth and get your schoolbags."

"Don't want to go to school," Danny whined, just like every other morning.

"Well, tomorrow you won't have to, will you?" coaxed my mother. "Tomorrow we'll be going on a lovely walk."

"Eo ork," gurgled Leo, which translated means, Leo walk.

"Clever boy!" Mum cried. "Who's Mummy's clever-wever boy, den?"

Ours is not an intellectual household.

"Tory, could you just . . ." my mother began.

"Got to dash!" I interrupted before she could list a dozen tasks for me to complete by eight-fifteen. "So much to catch up with at school."

"Of course, darling," Mum agreed. "You must be a bit behind with work after three days."

Work was the last thing on my mind.

"Ask her!" Ella prodded me in the ribs during attendance.

"Why me?"

"Because," said Pippa patiently, "you're the one who overheard the conversation."

I nodded, although my mind was elsewhere. Every time I looked at Ella, I thought about the other conversation I'd overheard.

"Tory?" Ella nudged me. "Will you or won't you?"

"Okay, but not here—I'll do it on the way to Maths. She might not say much if we're all ogling her."

As it happened, Maths was over and we were on our way to the Art block before I worked out the most tactful way of raising the subject.

"So you're not coming tomorrow, then," I began,

shoving the swing door open with my shoulder.

"Don't be stupid, of course I'm coming!" She sounded very edgy. "Why on earth wouldn't I be?"

"Because you're going to see your dad," I replied. "Your mum told my mum."

Even Hannah couldn't hide the surprise in her face.

"She said that? What else did she tell her?"

So there was obviously more to tell. I shrugged my shoulders.

"Nothing much," I murmured. "So why did you tell us you didn't even know where your dad was?"

Hannah's face relaxed.

"I didn't—not till Monday, when he got in touch with my mother," she said. "Apparently, he's suddenly decided he wants to see us and Mum's been taken in by it."

"But that's great," I began, as we crossed the school yard.

"No, it's not great at all!" Hannah snapped. "He says he's not my dad, walks out, and then expects me to go running the moment he snaps his fingers. Like I'm really going to do that!"

"But surely, if . . ."

"Leave it, okay?" Hannah thundered, so loudly

that several people turned to stare. "It's none of your business."

"So where's he been all this time?" I tried one more angle.

"I don't know and I don't care!" she shouted. "What's with all the questions, anyway?"

"Sorry," I said. "Glad you can come, anyway. Oh, and did I tell you Alex is bringing a load of his mates?"

Her shoulders relaxed and she grinned.

"I know, he told me. . . ."

Alarm bells rang.

"He told you? When?"

Hannah pushed open the door of the junior art room and dumped her bag on the floor.

"I met him in the lift and . . ."

"I know that," I said hastily. "And thanks for giving him my address. But when did he tell you . . . ?"

"After he'd gone, I worried myself sick about telling him where you lived," she said. "I thought your mum might go ballistic—you know, after the business about the bowling."

"She was fine about it," I assured her.

"Really?" It might have been my imagination, but Hannah sounded almost disappointed. "Oh well, that's good, then. When I spoke to Alex last night, I told him you were crazy about him. . . ."

"You spoke—you said what?"

My mind was racing.

"Well, it's true—I couldn't tell a lie, could I?"

I'm not sure whether she was having a go or not. And since Mrs. Cutler was waving paintbrushes in the air and ordering everyone to look at a pile of moldy fruit, I decided to give her the benefit of the doubt.

"Hey, listen to this!" Ella tossed her banana skin into the bin and pointed to the horoscope page of her new *Heaven Sent* magazine.

"'This is the week when a dream comes true,'" she read. "'With Venus and Mars working hard for you, new experiences come thick and fast, and if you play your cards right, you will discover that love conquers all!'"

She looked up, her face glowing.

"Isn't that just so cool? Do you think it means that Steven and I will get together tomorrow?"

"Do you have to keep on about Steven?" Pippa blurted out. "I'm getting sick of all this talk about boys."

"Could it be you're jealous?" Ella teased.

"No, I'm bloody not!" Pippa jumped to her feet, tossed her cola can into the bin, and stormed out of the cafeteria.

We looked at one another, totally gobsmacked. Pippa didn't do moods—of all of us, she was the calm and logical one.

"I'll go after her," I said. "See if she's okay."

"Hang on," Ella said. "I'll see what her horoscope says."

"For heaven's sake, Ella," I snapped. "Leave it out!"

All the jangly feelings I'd had all day came to the surface. I couldn't bear it—I knew that within a couple of days, all Ella's dreams would be shattered, and that the only new experiences she was going to get would be bad ones. And I couldn't get my mind off the fact that Hannah had been chatting to Alex the night before. What if he fancied her? And what if Hannah saying I was crazy about him actually put him off?

"I was just going to check whether . . ." Ella began, giving me an odd look.

"How can you say you believe in God one minute, and then swallow that load of drivel?"

I couldn't believe it was me speaking. There was a tightness in my chest and I felt like I was going to explode. And it wasn't even that time of the month.

"God created the stars and planets, didn't he?" Ella said calmly. "People have studied astrology since forever."

"That doesn't mean that a stupid magazine column means anything," I persisted. "It's just . . ."

"You were happy enough to go along with it when we were trying to catch Hannah out," interrupted Christy. "You weren't on your moral high horse then, were you?"

She doesn't say a lot, but when she does, it's pretty much spot on.

"Oh—just leave it!" I dumped my plate on the trolley and went in search of Pippa. This was horrible; we were all snappy with one another, and yet no one but me realized that within a few weeks, Ella would be gone and everything would be different.

I found Pippa just before attendance, sitting on one of the benches by the tennis courts.

"Are you okay?" I asked.

Pippa sighed.

"Yes, sorry about the outburst," she said. "It's just that—oh, I don't know. Things seem to be changing—we used to have such a laugh. . . ."

"We still do," I replied, pushing the thoughts of Ella's departure from my mind. "There's the walk tomorrow and . . ."

"With Hannah tagging along," sighed Pippa. "I don't know what it is about her, but I get the feeling that for as long as she's around, things will keep going wrong."

"Well, we won't let them," I said decisively. "She can't do any more harm, after all. We've wised up to her."

"I guess." Pippa didn't sound convinced. "But honestly, I think we should have a plan—you know, to deal with the next dumb thing she chucks at us."

"You and your plans!" I teased. "I reckon you'll end up as a politician."

"No way—I'm going to be a doctor, only I hope I don't get patients like Hannah because I might throttle them!"

I was relieved to hear her joking again.

"Anyway, let's change the subject," she said. "What are we going to do after the walk? Ella was talking about a barbecue again, like the one last year . . ."

"When Christy set fire to the hedge and your

dad had to get the hose," I giggled. "The latest idea is that we all go swimming and have a picnic down at White Rock."

"Really?" Pippa brightened. "That's not like Ella—she doesn't like getting her hair wet."

"Between you and me, I think she wants to appear in her new bikini—she thinks Steven . . ."

The expression on Pippa's face prevented me from going on.

"Will you teach me to snorkel?" I said rapidly. "I've never got the hang of it."

"It's easy!" Pippa said, brightening visibly. "And I'll bring the Frisbee and a beach ball."

She turned to me.

"It'll be a laugh, right?"

"Right!" I grinned. "It'll be a blast."

The atmosphere was somewhat uneasy at afternoon break. In fact, for once, I was glad Hannah was around, because the way she was rabbiting on, no one had to worry about the fact that Ella wasn't looking at Pippa and Pippa was trying doubly hard to make up for lunchtime.

"Anyway," Hannah said, "what are the plans for tomorrow?"

"We're all meeting at my house at nine-fifteen in the morning," Christy said. "My mother's one of the marshals."

"She is?" Pippa gasped.

"I know, I know, it wasn't my idea." Christy smiled. "Tory's dad persuaded her. She'll probably send half the people the wrong way, or lose the checklist or something."

"So where shall we start?" I asked. There are always six start points, to stop things getting too crowded.

"Mum's marshaling at the Lido," Christy said. "She can drop us there."

"I'll meet you there," Hannah cut in hastily. "I won't be able to get to Christy's that early. I've got the dentist at eight-forty-five."

"Poor you," murmured Christy. "Dentists freak me out."

"And don't forget to wear swimsuits under your shorts," Ella ordered us. "And bring food and drink and games for the beach and . . ."

"Hang on!" Pippa interrupted, and then immediately softened her tone. "That's a brilliant idea, Ella, but we can't carry all that stuff for twenty kilometers."

"We won't have to," Christy chipped in. "Mum says we can dump it all in our beach hut and collect it later."

"So that's all sussed!" Ella said. "We are going to have the best day ever."

✳ 11 ✳
Walk On By?

"**Where is she?**" Ella tapped her foot in irritation. "This is ridiculous—if she's not here in five minutes, we're leaving! I'm not wasting another minute of my birthday hanging about for her!"

"Who are we waiting for?" Steven asked, glancing at his watch as he tightened the laces on his Rollerblades.

"Hannah," I sighed. "I don't get it—she phoned me three times last night to check the arrangements."

"She's got a dentist's appointment," Alex interjected, spinning on his blades. "Maybe she's running late."

My heart lurched.

"How did you know?" I said, rather more abruptly than I had intended. It was bad enough that I couldn't Rollerblade, because if Alex was going to be speeding ahead like a maniac with all his mates, I was hardly likely to get to spend any time with him. Thankfully, only the first two kilo-meters were paved; after that, blading would be out. That thought might have cheered me up, but to be honest, I was just a bit miffed that Alex was clearly up to speed with Hannah's movements—I mean, I wanted her to be mates with the gang but preferably not with that one particular member of the gang.

"How did you know?" I asked again, when Alex didn't answer.

"She told me last night, on the phone," he said.

I would have asked a whole lot more, but Pippa cut in.

"This is crazy," she said. "There's no point in waiting."

"I'll call her," I said, pulling my mobile from the pocket of my shorts and punching in the number.

It rang and rang but there was no reply.

"That does it then!" Ella declared, waving her entry form in the air. "We're going!"

"Christina! Christina! Is time you begin walking now!"

Christy's mother, dressed incongruously in a scarlet velvet caftan, suede boots, and a cloche hat, came striding toward us from the table marked

Lido Checkpoint, waving her list in the air. She was purple in the face, which considering the temperature was in the high 70s, was hardly surprising.

"These are your badges," she declared, handing us a fistful of orange stickers. "You hand them in when you finish—it's for the security check."

We pinned them on dutifully under her watchful gaze.

"Now—you walk! Go, go!"

"Okay, Mum, cool it!" Christy muttered.

"This is your start time, no?" her mother retorted. "It is on my list. From the official starter person. 9:58! So go!"

"We're waiting for Hannah," Christy began.

"No, we are not!" Ella declared, linking arms with Steven. "We're off! Come on, Pippa."

"You have the key to the hut, yes?" Christy's mother yelled after us. "And a handkerchief? And the phone? And . . ."

Christy sighed. "Mothers. You'd think we were going up the Amazon, not for a walk through rural Sussex."

"You went without me!"

We had just passed the second checkpoint by the

Marina, when Hannah came belting up to us, red-faced and close to tears.

"How could you do that, Tory?" she cried as though leaving had been all down to me.

"We waited for ages," Pippa said reasonably. "And Tory phoned you but you didn't answer."

Hannah poked her hand in the pocket of her jeans.

"Oh no! I forgot my phone!" she wailed. "Anyway, you could have hung on a bit longer. I thought I was never going to find you."

"Well, you have found us, so let's get a move on!" Pippa declared, looking at the instructions. "Next stop—the coast guard's hut at the top of the cliff path!"

"Where are Ella and the others?" Hannah asked, wiping her nose on the back of her hand and falling in step beside us.

"Way ahead," I muttered grumpily. To make matters worse, Mark had lent Ella his blades and she was off with Steven and Alex, giggling and oh-so-accidentally falling into Steven's arms. All right, I admit it. I was jealous.

Christy grinned, squeezing my arm. "Don't worry, they'll have to stop blading once we're up on the cliffs and going through the fields. So you'll get Alex's undivided attention."

"It doesn't bother me," I assured her. She didn't look convinced.

"So was your mum okay about you coming today?" I asked Hannah, walking as fast as I could along the narrow path to catch up with Ella and the guys, who were perched on a stile waiting for the rest of us.

"No," Hannah replied curtly, dodging ahead of a couple smooching their way along the path. "We had a huge row about it, actually."

"But you won!" Christy said, panting behind us as we reached the stile and dumped our rucksacks on the ground.

"And you can always go another weekend, right?" I added.

I thought I was being polite, nice, conciliatory, whatever you want to call it.

"No, I bloody well can't!" Hannah shouted and then burst into tears.

"Oh, for God's sake, don't start again!" I shouldn't have said that—I knew it the moment the words were out—but I was fed up with Hannah's histrionics.

Even then, if it had stopped there, it would all have been fine. But Ella was looking at me like thunder.

"Leave it out, Tory," she snapped.

It was such a stupid little thing, but Ella being off with me was the last straw. I couldn't stop thinking that within a few weeks, she might be gone and I wanted everything to be perfect between us. If Hannah hadn't been with us, it would have been.

"Are you okay, Hannah?" Alex asked in that embarrassed kind of way guys have when girls get emotional.

Hannah nodded and flashed him a brighter smile than the rest of us ever got.

"Sorry," she said. "I just get upset about things— you know. . . ."

"It's okay," Alex said. "After what you told me, I'm not surprised."

So she'd been whining to him too, had she? And probably saying that I was mean and unkind and didn't understand her. Or was that just my conscience nagging me?

Hannah sniffed and smiled wanly.

"Sorry—it's just that it's been a bad few days. Pathetic, I know . . ."

"No, it's not," Alex said. "Want a peppermint?"

I suppose, looking back, that was the turning point. I didn't say any more there and then; I just seethed quietly inside. We looked at the route and Pippa read out the things we had to collect—the time of high tide at White Rock, a load of different flowers, the name of the church-warden at Ovenden church—and we all headed off. The trouble was that as soon as we reached the tarmac path, the guys all went ahead, and Alex didn't turn around to check where I was. Not once.

Ella was as miffed as me, because Mark had taken his blades back and so she was stuck with us while Steven was at least three-quarters of a kilo-meter ahead.

"Okay, stop!" she panted about ten minutes later. "I've got an idea!"

"What's that?" I asked, still trying to put things right between us.

"We cut across this field, right?" She pointed through the trees to a wide expanse of farmland. "That way, we'll be ahead of the guys, because they've got to stick to the path and go right round those two farms."

"No way!" Hannah gasped. "Absolutely, posi-tively not."

"Why not?" Ella demanded.

"I think it's a great idea," I said at once. "It will save us at least half a kilometer, if not more."

"Cows!" wailed Hannah. "Can't you see? Loads of them."

"So?" Ella sounded irritated. "If we do it my way, we can wait for the guys to catch up and then I can . . ."

"Smooch with Steve." Pippa laughed.

Ella poked her in the ribs but she didn't deny that Pippa had a point.

"I'm scared of cows," Hannah said.

"They're harmless," Pippa protested. "They're more scared of you than you are of them. Come on."

She began climbing over the five-barred gate into the field, Ella hard on her heels.

"I can't do it!" Hannah whined.

"Well," I suggested as calmly as I could, "you go 'round the path and we'll go across the field. Sorted!"

"Not on my own!" Hannah protested. "That's so not fair because I don't know the way like you do and anyway, remember my mum said . . ."

That did it.

"Whine, whine, whine!" I snapped. "That's all you ever do, isn't it? What are you going to do? Run to Mummy and tell tales!"

"No, I . . ."

"You think you're so hard done by—well, let me tell you, there are people here with far more to complain about than you've got!"

"I doubt it." Hannah's face was frozen, but her voice was calm.

"Well, you would, wouldn't you?"

"Tory, leave it, it's not worth it." Christy touched my arm but I was in full flood.

"You think you're so hard done by. What about Ella . . . ?"

I just managed to swallow back the words.

". . . and her idea? Couldn't you just do something for someone else for a change?"

It was a feeble end to my diatribe, but I was just thankful that I hadn't let slip the news about Ella moving.

"That does it!" Hannah said bursting into tears. "I've had enough of you and your beastliness. First you accuse me of lying, and now, just because I'm trying to be brave. . . ."

"You? Brave?" Later, Pippa would say it was all down to my hormones (she's very into bodily cycles, what with wanting to be a doctor) but frankly I knew I was just being plain nasty.

"Stop it, you two!" Pippa shouted from the other side of the gate. "We're wasting precious time, okay? Now, come on, Hannah, I'll walk with you and shoo the cows away."

"Forget it!" Hannah turned on her heel and began running back down the path, dodging walkers who eyed her in surprise. "I'm going home!"

"Now look what you've done, Tory!" Christy grumbled. "I'll go after her."

"No, leave her." Ella hadn't said a word since my outburst but now she hitched her rucksack onto her back and clambered over the gate. "Tory's right— we can do without her incessant moaning."

A wave of relief flooded over me. At least Ella wasn't holding anything against me.

"You know, don't you?" Ella turned to me as Pippa and Christy ran on ahead, muttering under their breaths and shooing cows out of our path.

"Know what?" I hesitated, not wanting to cause any more damage.

"About what's happening—us moving and every-thing," she said.

"So they told you?"

"No. They haven't said a word to my face. They must think I'm stupid—I've been listening in on their late-night conversations for days."

"It's going to be so awful," I said. "Nothing will be the same without you."

"I'm only moving house, silly," she replied. "It's not like I'm going to the ends of the earth."

She faltered.

"Unless . . . do you know something I don't?"

She held my gaze.

"No, of course I don't. I just meant . . ."

"Tory. This is me, okay."

And because it was Ella, I found I couldn't lie.

"I probably got it wrong. . . ." I began.

"Tell me."

So I did. I told her what I'd heard, and I watched the color drain from Ella's face and saw her struggling not to cry.

"That's why I went ballistic at Hannah," I admit-ted. "She's got it made compared with you. And she's here and you'll be gone and . . ."

Ella looked at me.

"It won't happen," she said. "We won't be leaving Westbeach."

"Your parents changed their mind?" I gasped, my heart lifting.

"I don't know," she said. "But my horoscope says it's going to be a really good year and if I had to leave, it wouldn't be, so that's that."

Hearing her talk like that made me want to cry. She could pretend to be as brave as she liked, but I knew how she was feeling.

She jutted her chin out and looked at me defiantly.

"I know you think I'm stupid," she said, "but I do believe in positive thinking. If I believe it'll be okay, it will be."

I sighed, but thought better of arguing.

I smiled. "Let's hope you're right. I guess I was a bit strong with Hannah, though."

Ella shook her head.

"No, she deserved it," she said with a sigh. "Anyway, no harm done."

Over the next hour, things got better. Ella was friends again and was ambling along in front with Steve, and Alex had hung back waiting for me.

Mind you, his opening question when we met up again didn't do much for my general feeling of well-being.

"Where's Hannah?" he'd asked, pulling a face as a whiff of cow dung wafted up from my muddy trainers.

"She got fed up and left," I told him. "My fault, I guess."

"How do you work that out?" he asked, slipping a hand into mine.

I would have answered at once, but the feel of his hand in mine seemed to rob me of the power of speech for at least thirty seconds. I took a deep breath.

"I had a go at her for whining and it got out of control," I admitted. "I know it was rotten of me— I guess I'm not a very nice person."

"I think you are," Alex said in the kind of matter-of-fact way that prevented me from asking him to repeat it. "Anyway, don't let's talk about her."

He turned to me.

"I'd rather talk about us," he said in a rush, his face turning red and his eyes scanning the horizon as if he'd seen something hugely fascinating. "I'm sorry we got off on the wrong foot."

"We did?" What had I done wrong now, I wondered.

"Hannah said that you couldn't stand boys that came on too strong after one date," he began. "And I don't usually do that, but . . ."

"Hang on, hang on!" I butted in. "Hannah told *me* that you don't like girls who come on strong. . . ."

"I never said that!" he gasped. "Where did she get that idea from?"

"You'd be surprised the ideas she gets," I said ruefully.

"So—I haven't blown it, then? With you, I mean?"

He looked so sweet and so anxious that I wanted to kiss him, but I managed to restrain myself.

"No, of course not," I replied meekly.

"And I've got a confession to make," he said. "About the hair clip thing I got you. . . ."

"It's lovely," I babbled. "The reason I'm not wearing it is because . . ."

"I didn't buy it," he blurted out. "It was my sister's."

"What? You pinched it?"

He shook his head.

"No—I told her I'd met this really cool girl and

I needed an excuse to go and see her and—well, it was her idea."

He blushed.

"And then, when Hannah told me that you are really anti-boys, and hate fuss, I reckoned you would be thinking I was a total dweeb."

"I am not anti-boys!" I protested. "If anything, boys are anti-me."

He grinned. "This one isn't."

And then he kissed me.

"You don't mind?"

I shook my head because the power of speech had temporarily left me.

So he did it again.

❋ 12 ❋

It Wasn't Meant to Be Like This

"**One hundred forty-five pounds,** sixty-five," Pippa announced, having scribbled a load of figures on the back of her chocolate wrapper. "That's what we four have raised—of course, that's without Hannah's money."

"Speaking of Hannah," I said, "don't you think we should try and find out what's happened to her?"

My conscience was beginning to kick in.

"Ring her if it makes you feel better," Christy suggested as she unlocked the beach hut to retrieve our things.

"She didn't have her mobile with her, remember," I sighed, grabbing my beach bag. "I could try her home number, I guess."

I pulled my phone from my pocket and found the little envelope flashing on the screen to say a message had arrived. I guess that because the phone was on vibrate I hadn't noticed.

"Oh, whoops!" I gasped as I scanned the message.

"What's up?" Ella asked, slapping sun cream on to her arms.

"TORY, HANNAH'S PHONE SWITCHED OFF," I read out loud. "PLEASE GET HER 2 RING ME URGENTLY. ANGELA."

We looked at one another.

"Now what do we do?" I asked. "I can hardly ring Mrs. Soper and say we've lost Hannah."

"You could say she went off in a huff," suggested Pippa, tightening the strap on her snorkel.

We all looked at her.

"Then again, perhaps not," she added.

"Try her home number," Christy suggested.

"Her mum will have done that," I retorted. "Still, no harm trying, I suppose."

I punched it in and waited.

No reply.

"Maybe she's calmed down and she's on the beach, waiting for us," Pippa said, shading her eyes from the sun and looking across the sea wall to the pebble beach. "Let's go."

The guys were already in the water, larking

about, but there was no sign of Hannah.

"Come on in!" Steven shouted to Ella. "Bring the Frisbee!"

Ella slipped off her shorts and began heading down the beach, wincing as the pebbles cut into her feet.

"Hang on," I called after her. "What shall I do? Shall I phone her mum back?"

Ella shook her head.

"Just pretend your mobile was switched off all day," she shouted to me. "That way, you wouldn't have read the message, would you? No one can blame you for that."

"Good one, Ella!" Pippa said approvingly, pulling off her T-shirt. "Go on, Tory, switch it off now. Then she can't bother us again."

"But what if . . ."

"Come on, Tory! It's great in here!" Alex shouted, leaping over a breaking wave.

I switched the phone off.

"Great!" said Pippa. "Problem solved."

Alex was lying on the beach beside me, tickling my nose with a feather he'd found on the shoreline, when Ella nudged my arm.

"Tory! Isn't that your dad?"

Alex sat up in alarm. I propped myself up on my elbow and peered up the beach. Dad was stumbling down across the stones, calling my name.

"Where's Hannah?" he demanded, scanning the beach and realizing she wasn't with us.

"She—she decided to leave," I began.

"Leave? When?"

I swallowed hard.

"I'm not sure—one o'clock, half past, something like that."

He looked at his watch.

"And now it's five-thirty," he stated. "Did she say where she was going?"

I swallowed hard.

"Home, I think." I tried to sound very casual about it all.

"Well, she's not there," he said in the tone of voice that made my stomach do a double flip. "So why did she leave?"

I had known the crunch question would come eventually.

"I . . . she . . . we . . ."

"She was in a grump," Pippa chimed in. "She and Tory had words, and she threw a wobbly and marched off."

"And no one went after her?" My father sounded incredulous that we could be so unfeeling.

"Hannah's like that," Ella chipped in. "She's just one of those people who is always whining about something. She said she was fed up and was going home—it wasn't up to us to stop her."

"Not only is she not at home," my father continued, "but she hasn't handed in her security badge."

"She probably just forgot," Christy said, but I could tell she was feeling as guilty as I was.

"Shall Steven and I go and look for her, sir?" Alex asked respectfully, jumping to his feet. "We've got blades so we can get around pretty fast."

"That's kind," my father said.

"We'll go too," I began, but my father had other ideas.

"I think you'd better come home, Tory," my dad said. "Hannah's mum's just got back from London and she's not happy."

He pulled me to my feet.

"In fact," he went on, "I think you should all go back to your own homes—just in case Hannah turns up at one of your houses, or phones you."

He surveyed us all solemnly.

"This could," he said, "prove to be very serious."

"Have you been bullying Hannah again?" Mrs. Soper was on her feet before I'd got through the kitchen door. "Because if you have . . ."

"Now, Angela dear, calm down," my mother said. "I'm sure Tory hasn't done anything of the sort."

"We did have a bit of a row," I began.

"I knew it!" Angela thumped the table with her fist. "Hannah's been so forgiving, so patient with you girls and this is what happens!"

I knew better than to say a word but I wanted to tell her that if anyone had been patient, it was me.

"If something's happened to Hannah," she went on, "I'll never ever forgive you!"

I felt sick. Why were they all assuming I was the bad guy? Okay, so maybe I'd been a bit mean, but they didn't know what it was like, having Hannah going on and on, and knowing that the parents wanted us to be mates, even though we had virtually nothing in common.

"I'm sure nothing's happened," my father said quietly. "Now, let's just get the facts, shall we? Just what happened, Tory?"

"You abandoned her again, didn't you?" Angela cried. "You and your gang. Just like at the pier."

"The pier?" my mother frowned. "You left Hannah at the pier?"

"No. Yes—it wasn't like that," I mumbled.

"I think, Victoria," my father said, "you'd better tell us what it was like."

"We were going on the dodgem cars, and we asked Hannah to come, and she said that Mum had said we couldn't . . ."

"Which I had," my mother reminded me. I began to wonder whose side she was on.

". . . and so she decided to stay on the pier and we went."

I knew I was for the high jump, but this wasn't the time for anything but the truth.

"Typical!" Angela stormed. "That is so cruel."

"Stupid, maybe," my mother interrupted calmly. "But hardly cruel."

She paused and looked at Angela long and hard.

"Hannah took photos that night, didn't she?" she asked.

Angela nodded.

"She got the camera for her birthday," she said. "Not that I see what that's got to do with it."

"A very elaborate one, is it?" Mum persisted.

"Darling, I hardly see . . ." my father began, but

Mum gave him one of her looks and he shut up.

"No, very basic," Angela said.

"Telephoto lens?" Mum asked.

"What—at the price they cost? What's all this about?"

Mum smiled.

"Just that Hannah took photos of Tory and the others on the dodgem cars," she said. "Lovely, they were—really good."

"She's very good with a camera," Angela said, slightly mollified.

"But of course, to get those close-ups, she would have to have left the pier and gone to the funfair," Mum concluded calmly. "So she wasn't left behind, was she?"

I could have hugged my mother on the spot. I would never have cottoned on to that.

"I expect," Mum murmured, "that like any normal fourteen-year-old, she decided that fun mattered more than rules. You can't blame her."

"I—well, yes, she probably . . ."

Angela collected herself.

"That's not the point," she gabbled. "The point is—where is Hannah now! Tory, you said you had a row with her."

She made it sound as if I had committed murder.

"Things just piled up," I said. "She was late for the walk, so we left without . . ."

"How mean!"

". . . we'd tried phoning but there was no reply and then we got to this field and it was full of cows and she wouldn't walk through it . . ."

"Well, of course not! She hates animals," Angela butted in.

"And she kept going on and on about how awful things were, and about her dad. . . ."

"She spoke about her father?" Angela gasped. "What did she say?"

"I can't remember," I lied. "I mean she's been talking about him off and on for weeks, about how he deserted her and, honestly, we do feel sorry for her and we did try . . ."

I could feel the tears welling up inside me and I struggled desperately to contain them.

"She said that?" Angela was staring at me. "He deserted her?"

I nodded.

"And I got cross—which I know was mean and I'm sorry—but I was upset about Ella leaving and . . ."

That did it. The thought of Ella—and the realization that I'd dropped myself in it even deeper by mentioning her secret, made the tears flow. Mum reached out her hand, put her finger to her lips, and said nothing.

"Hannah just got mad at me and ran off," I finished lamely.

To my horror, Angela put her head in her hands and began to cry.

"That's what she did with me this morning," she sobbed. "At the station."

My mother stood up and bustled over to the stove.

"I'll make tea," she said. Mum always makes tea in a crisis, even if it's the last thing you want.

"I thought she was at the dentist this morning," I said.

"The dentist? What on earth gave you that idea?" Angela asked.

"Hannah said so," I said. "That's why she didn't want to meet us at Christy's place."

For the first time, Angela looked at me with something other than out-and-out hatred.

"There was never a dental appointment," she said. "I'd finally persuaded her to come to London with me to see her father. Then, just as we were buying the tickets, she said she wasn't coming."

"I see," my father murmured. I'm quite sure he didn't, but he probably felt he had to say something.

"We had a bit of a shouting match in the station lobby, and she said she was fed up with me, fed up with the lies. . . ."

"Lies?" My mother turned, kettle poised under the tap.

"Her father's lies, I mean." Angela seemed confused and agitated. "She said she'd had enough and was going off with her friends."

"You don't think," I began, clutching at straws, "that she wished she had gone with you, and so when she ran off, she decided to get on a train and go and see him?"

"It's possible," my mother urged. "After all, it's only fifty minutes to London on a fast train. Why don't you ring her father and check?"

"Because I know it's the one place she won't be," Angela said.

"You can't know for sure," my father commented. "Kids change their minds like the wind."

Angela sighed and chewed her lip.

"I haven't been totally honest with you," she said. "The reason I know Hannah won't be with her father is because . . ."

At that very moment, Ben hurtled into the kitchen, followed closely by Danny.

"We're hungry!" Ben said.

"Starving, actually," added Danny.

"Go to the freezer, get two ice creams, and go back upstairs," Mum ordered, dumping the kettle on the stove. You could see that the boys thought Christmas had come. They didn't make another sound, but scooted off before she could change her mind.

"You were saying?" Mum repeated, turning to Angela.

She paused and eyed me doubtfully.

"Tory, go upstairs," Mum ordered, but Angela shook her head.

"No, let her stay. She might as well hear it all." She bit her lip. "Then she might be a bit kinder to Hannah."

I swallowed hard to stop myself from answering back.

"Hannah can't go to see her dad on her own, unannounced—because Kevin's in prison."

Angela's hand began to shake. My father, who is

trained in these kinds of things, sat down beside her and patted her arm.

"Oh—Angela!" Mum cried. "I had no idea."

The events of the past few weeks reeled through my mind like a videotape on fast forward.

"Does Hannah know?" The question may have sounded silly, but I had to get my head straight.

"Of course she knows!" Angela wheeled round to face me. "How would I keep something like that from her, for heaven's sake?"

"It's just that she never said," I began.

"That's because I told her that no one must ever find out," her mother replied. "I thought it would be for the best."

It all began to fall into place. That's why Hannah had pretended he'd walked out. Because she didn't want anyone to know the truth.

"I mean, her dad didn't kill anyone or anything," Angela went on hurriedly. "It was—fraud. But the shame of it—we had to keep it secret."

"How awful for you!" Mum gasped. "Earl Grey or Darjeeling?"

"Earl Grey, thanks—he was very clever, even the police said that," Angela gabbled, and for a moment she sounded almost proud. "He hoodwinked so many people—stealing money from clients' accounts, raising false invoices and . . . I can't talk about it."

"Why didn't you tell us, my dear?" my father asked. "We could have helped in some way. . . ."

"How?" Angela snapped. "Prayed for him? I'm sorry—oh, Douglas, I'm sorry, that was rude of me, it's just . . ."

"It's all right," my dad said soothingly. "This is very distressing for you."

"And now Hannah's disappeared," Angela sobbed. "What if something's happened to her? You hear such awful things about young girls being snatched and . . ."

"I'm sure she's fine," my mother stressed. "She's probably just taking time out, having a bit of personal space."

"Although if she doesn't turn up soon, we should inform the police," Dad said softly. "It's nearly seven o'clock."

At the mention of the police, Angela wailed even more.

"Toby's out looking for her—maybe she's phoned him. I'll give him another call."

She punched in some numbers on her mobile phone.

"Toby? It's me. Any news?"

The way her face crumpled told us all we needed to know.

"You will keep looking, won't you?" she pleaded. "And keep checking the flat, okay? Promise?"

"Toby's the last person she'd go to," I butted in as she rang off. "She can't stand him; she said that if you two get married—"

"Married? Are you insane?" Angela looked horrified.

"Sorry, I didn't mean to be rude. . . ."

"Toby's half my age, Tory. And he's gay. Strikes me you have far too vivid an imagination!"

That's when I lost it. Big time.

"That is so not on!" I shouted. "It wasn't my idea—Hannah said you two were an item."

Mrs. Soper almost dropped her teacup.

"Hannah told you that? You're not making it up?"

"I swear with my life, on the Bible," I said. "Cross my heart and—"

"Yes, Tory, we get the message," my father interjected. He's very against swearing, biblical or otherwise.

I guess I should have shut up there and then, but I didn't.

"What was I supposed to do?" I shouted. "Accuse Hannah of lying when she told me things? Actually, yes—that would have been a good idea. Because the one thing Hannah is good at is lying. That, and making trouble for other people!"

"Tory!" My father stepped forward and threw me a warning look. I ignored him.

"We should have been told about her dad—I mean, you don't know what it's been like. Hannah's been causing all sorts of trouble, and we tried to be nice because Mum and you are friends, although why that should matter . . ."

"Tory!"

"And if we'd known the truth, we might have been nicer to her and made allowances and she wouldn't be missing and . . ."

I couldn't go on. I just sat there and sobbed.

"Right," my father declared, "I think this has gone on long enough. I'll call the police."

That just made me cry even more. I had visions of Hannah lying in a ditch, or kidnapped by some maniac.

Mrs. Soper touched my hand.

"I'm sorry, Tory," she murmured. "I was out of

order. Hannah should never have said those things—I'll be having words with her when . . ."

Her voice faltered.

"If only I hadn't said anything to her," I sobbed. "I didn't mean to upset her—I just wanted everything to be perfect and she wouldn't take the shortcut across the field and the boys were getting farther and farther ahead . . ."

"Boys?" began my mother.

". . . and when she ran off, we just thought she'd go straight home."

"Tory, don't!" Angela stretched out a hand and took mine. "I'm sorry I blew my top. But listen, this is very important. Did Hannah tell you anything else, anything at all, that might give us a clue as to where she is?"

"I can't think of anything." I said. "I mean, she was upset about her dad not being her dad, but she never said she wanted to find her real one or anything like that."

"She told you what?"

I repeated my words.

"Oh, my God!"

Mrs. Soper clamped her hands to her face and closed her eyes.

"You did right." Angela's voice was a mere croak. "And Hannah would have hated for you to tell me anything—especially since it's all lies."

I opened my mouth to ask a question, but one look from my father made me shut it again.

"Where can she be?" Angela sobbed. "Half of me wants to wring her neck, the other half just wants to hold her in my arms."

She dabbed her eyes with a crumpled tissue.

"She hasn't been her normal self for weeks," she said. "She would never have been like this in the past—she even switched off her phone so that I couldn't reach her."

"No, she left the phone at home. She told us that when she caught up with us," I said.

Angela's eyes widened, and even Mum looked more anxious.

Angela gasped. "So—wherever she is, she doesn't have a phone? And I've been texting her and leaving voice mail messages all afternoon. I just know something's happened."

That's when I remembered that my phone was still switched off. I was desperate to text Ella and the others and keep them up to date, so I mouthed to Mum that I needed the loo and scuttled out of the room.

The moment I switched my phone on, the text messages hurtled in thick and fast.

ANY NEWS? NOTHING MY END, LOL
ELLA
R U OK? HOPE U R NOT IN 2 MUCH
TROUBLE. PIPPA

Then, just as I was washing my hands, the phone bleeped again.

NEW MESSAGE

It was Alex.
And what I read blew my mind.

I took a deep breath and shut the loo door behind me. As my hand rested on the kitchen doorknob, I heard Angela's voice.

"You see, it hit Hannah really badly when Kev was caught with his finger in the till, so to speak," she was saying. "She screamed at him and said she had criminal blood in her veins because of her genetic makeup."

She laughed weakly.

"They'd been doing DNA and stuff at school," she said, heaving a sigh.

I knew I should go in at once and tell her the news, but something held me back.

"And then—that's when he told her that he wasn't her father?" my mother queried.

"No, you've got it all wrong!" Angela was almost shouting. "All Kev said—and remember, he was facing prison at the time—was . . ."

She paused.

"Let me get the right words. He said, 'I suppose you'd prefer it if I wasn't your dad.' And that's when Hannah screamed at him and said that from that moment on, as far as she was concerned, he wasn't."

My heart was actually pounding. It was like watching a really gripping thriller on TV—only this time it was for real.

"Children often react badly at first," my father started as I pushed open the kitchen door.

"Not just children." Angela sighed. "I told her that we'd move house, that we'd start again, and that no one need ever know the truth. In fact, I went further—I made her promise that she wouldn't speak about the past to anyone. I thought that would help her. But now Kevin's ill with worry—he loves her so much and . . ."

Her voice cracked.

". . . for all I know she might be dead!"

"She's not dead," I said, looking to my mother for support. "She's okay—she's at Alex's house."

My voice was shaking, and it wasn't just from relief that Hannah was in one piece. I couldn't believe that Hannah would make up all those stories about her mum getting pregnant—and that we'd been taken in by them.

Angela leaped to her feet and burst into tears.

"She's okay, she's not hurt?"

"Well—she's got a few cuts and bruises apparently, and Alex's mum wanted to take her to the emergency room, but Hannah said she wanted you."

"I'll go to her now—oh, thank God—but cuts and bruises, what happened?" She was grabbing her bag and running her fingers through her hair and looking completely at sea.

"I'll drive you, Angela," my father said, immediately taking control. "Debbie, you phone Toby and tell him Hannah's safe. And Tory, you'd better let your friends know."

He picked up his car keys and ushered Angela out the door. The moment they'd gone, I burst into tears.

"It's all my fault," I sobbed. "Why am I turning into such a horrid person, Mum? If I hadn't yelled at Hannah, she wouldn't have run off and got hurt. Supposing she fell over a cliff or something?"

"Darling, be reasonable," Mum said softly. "If she'd done that, she would have something rather more serious than a few cuts. What exactly did Alex say?"

I handed her my phone with the saved message.

HANNAH'S HERE. CRYING LOADS AND GOT BAD CUTS AND BRUISES. KEEPS ASKING TO C U. MUM WANTS 2 TAKE HER 2 HOSPITAL. H WONT GO. HER MUM NOT ANSWERING PHONE. ALEX. PS H KEEPS SAYING SORRY BUT WONT SAY 4 WHAT.

"I expect she fell over on the path when she was running away," Mum suggested. "Although, of course, it's been a long time. . . ."

"Whatever happened, it's my fault," I cried. "I

was so grumpy and jangly today and. . . ."

"Listen to me, Tory," Mum said. "Everyone has off days, everyone says things they regret later, but you've done one really good thing today."

"Like what?" I wasn't convinced.

"You told the whole truth," she said. "And it would seem that that is something neither Hannah nor her mum managed to do."

She gave me a hug.

"I'm really proud of you," she said. "And I'm sorry I nagged you to be friends with Hannah. It's not going to work, is it?"

I took a deep breath.

"No," I said, shaking my head. "I don't think it is."

❋ 13 ❋

That's What
Friends Are For

I woke up to the sound of my mobile phone
ringing. I don't know whether it was the relief of
everything being out in the open, but I'd slept like a
log, and when I glanced at the clock it was gone nine.

"I need to talk," Alex said. "Can I come over?"

"Of course," I cried, leaping out of bed. "That
would be great."

"Fine," he said and hung up. I wished he'd
sounded a bit more enthusiastic.

I hurtled into the shower, dried, dressed, decided
it looked all wrong, and was halfway through
pulling on my dead-cool silky trousers when the bell
rang. I heard Mum ushering Alex upstairs.

"How's Hannah?" Alex asked me.

I'm ashamed to say I felt a bit annoyed that she
was his main concern, and then hated myself for
being so selfish.

"Her mum says she's exhausted but all right," I said. "So what happened yesterday?"

"She turned up on the doorstep and her arms were cut and bleeding," he told me, the words pouring out as if they'd been bottled up for ages. "She said that she'd fallen over because she was blinded by tears after you laid into her."

I felt as if someone had stuck a knife in me.

"Of course, it was obviously a load of lies," he added calmly. "You don't fall over and have perfectly ungrazed knees and a whole load of five-centimeter cuts on your arms. And you don't hurt yourself at one o'clock and still bleed like crazy at half-past six. So clearly the cuts happened a lot later than when she left us."

He bit his lip.

"Thing is," he muttered, "I don't know what to do."

"About what?" I asked. "It's not like you were involved."

"But I am," he stressed. "See, when she arrived at my place, my mum and dad were in the garden, and she was crying and everything and threw herself into my arms."

I fought a battle against the wave of jealousy and anger that surged through me.

"She clung to me and said no one wanted her, and that I was the only person who'd been nice to her on the walk," he went on. "I was dead embarrassed and, to be honest, I pushed her away."

I tried not to let my relief show on my face.

"And when I did . . ."

"Yes?"

"I felt something sharp in her pocket."

I shrugged.

"So—what are you getting at? She must . . . oh my God."

"Exactly."

I felt sick. I'd read about that sort of thing, obviously—it's in all the problem pages of my magazines. But to think that someone I knew would actually . . . For a moment, I couldn't say a word. My eyes filled with tears.

"Poor Hannah," I whispered. "You have to tell someone."

"You think so?"

"I know so," I said. "For her sake, Alex. We have no choice."

It had been four days since we had seen Hannah. A huge "FOR SALE" board had gone up outside Ella's house, and Pippa had had a go at me for not telling her what was going on. If she had known the other secret I was hiding, she would have been doubly edgy.

"What shall we say?" Ella asked tentatively as we got the lift up to Hannah's flat.

"Just act natural," Pippa said firmly.

"And be nice," I urged, echoing the words we'd heard so often before. "She needs us."

"Oh, really?" Christy sounded unconvinced. "Why—so she can create a few more dramas and make our lives hell?"

The lift stopped, but I didn't move.

"Listen," I said to the three of them. "You have to trust me on this. There are things you don't know, and things I wish I didn't know."

"Like what?" Pippa's interest was instantly aroused, but I wasn't falling into that trap.

"I can't say," I said. "But you know I yelled at Hannah and told her that she wasn't as badly off as Ella? Well, I was wrong."

Ella eyed me closely.

"Us lot, we'll be fine no matter what happens to us," I continued, not quite sure where the words were coming from, but aware that they were, for once, the right ones. "Hannah—well, she might not be. So just be friendly. Please?"

Ella nodded.

"Okay, deal! Agreed?" She turned to the others.

"Agreed," they chorused. "Come on, let's go and be saintly before we change our minds."

"About Saturday," Hannah began after we'd given her the chocolates and the magazines we'd brought. "I need to tell you . . ."

"It's okay," Ella said. "We were bitchy and we're sorry. You don't have to talk about it."

"I must," Hannah said, taking a deep breath and fiddling with her fringe. "You know I ran off?"

We nodded.

"I didn't go home because I wanted to make you all suffer," she blurted out. "I thought if I stayed out all night, you'd be in the most awful trouble."

"But why would you want . . . ?" Christy began, but Pippa nudged her in the ribs and she shut up.

"Anyway," she said, ignoring the interruption, "I got so mad inside, because Mum had gone to see Dad and I wanted to, and yet I didn't want to . . . does that make sense?"

"Your mum had . . . ?" Pippa started, but stopped as I glared at her.

"Half of me wished he wasn't my father—that's why I lied to you," she went on, her voice catching as she fought back the tears. "And half of me missed him so much. . . ."

Her voice cracked and she took a deep breath. I could see that the others were getting more puzzled by the second.

"In the end, I just wanted to be able to tell you the whole truth, which Mum said was out of the question. . . ."

"We won't tell. . . ." Pippa began.

"Oh, it's okay now," Hannah said. "Mum knows it was stupid of both of us. Dad is in prison."

She articulated those last four words as if she were saying them for the first time. Pippa gasped, Christy's eyes bulged, and Ella bit her lip but, to their credit, no one said a word.

"And I guess I felt like I was to blame."

That was the crux of it and I knew it.

"Of course you weren't!" I burst out hastily. "You didn't do anything wrong."

"Mum and me spent loads of money on clothes, and used to get Dad to take us to posh places on holiday, and when he got caught he shouted and said that if he hadn't had us on his back, he wouldn't have had to cook the books to pay for our lavish lifestyle."

A tear trickled down her face.

"I thought he'd stopped loving me."

"And that's why you told everyone that he wasn't your dad, that he'd disappeared . . . is that it?" Pippa was cottoning on fast.

She nodded.

"I got so angry, every day," she said. "It was like this great big volcano inside me waiting to burst. When I was little, he used to punish me every time I told a lie . . ."

"So you did it way back then as well . . . ?" Christy began and then bit her tongue.

". . . and then after Tory yelled on Saturday, it was like everyone was against me."

"I'm so sorry. . . ." I began.

"Don't be," Hannah said. "Anyway, I ran off and ran and ran for what seemed like ages—not back to Westbeach, because I couldn't face seeing anyone I knew, and I knew all the walkers would be going back, so I went in the opposite direction."

We looked at one another, realizing just how

miserable she must have been.

"I sat on the rocks by the old lighthouse for a long time, thinking and trying to calm down. But all I could think about was how you were all so close to each other, and how you were getting boyfriends. . . ."

"Not me," Pippa interjected.

". . . and I just felt worse and worse."

"Then what happened?" Ella asked.

"That's when I decided to stay out and get you all worried," she admitted. "I walked back to Westbeach and saw you lot on the beach having a great time. That's when I flipped."

She hugged her arms round her body.

"Please don't hate me," she pleaded.

"Hannah, we don't hate you," I stressed. "And you don't need to say another word."

"Is that when you fell over?" Pippa asked. "Tory said you'd had a nasty fall—was it when you were running away from us?"

I held Hannah's gaze and gave the very faintest nod.

She looked at me and her eyes widened.

I nodded again.

"Yes," she said slowly, "So I went to Alex's—I do

fancy him a bit, sorry Tory, and . . . well, you know the rest."

At that point, Hannah's mum came in and we changed the subject. It was as we left that Hannah squeezed my hand.

"Thanks," she whispered. "Really. Thanks."

Epilogue

Dear Tory,

You just have to read this! I cut it out of my new local paper—it's quite a funky one for a sleepy seaside town like Hastings. Pretty interesting, isn't it? Have to dash—got a new Saturday job.

Love, Ella

SHELBY'S SPOT ON STAR SEARCH!
GEMINI

Oh boy, Gemini! When it comes to complicated summers, yours wins the prizes hands down! Right now, you're feeling that everything is up in the air—but then, you're an air sign, so what do you expect? Friends are on the move and you're feeling abandoned; but don't despair, there's a large dollop of romance heading straight your way. So start hitting the shops, kiddo, and grabbing yourself some funky gear—and don't let anyone hijack you. You're a caring soul and that's great—but the coming year is your time to show the world who you really are and stop worrying about what other people think. So go, girl, go!